CONTENTS

Pedigree

Published 2012.
Pedigree Books Limited, Beech Hill House,
Walnut Gardens, Exeter, Devon EX4 4DH
www.pedigreebooks.com
books@pedigreegroup.co.uk

© 2012 Pokémon.
© 1997–2012 Nintendo,
Creatures, GAME FREAK, TV
Tokyo, ShoPro, JR Kikaku.
Pokémon properties are
trademarks of Nintendo.

The Pedigree trademark, email and website
addresses, are the sole and exclusive
properties of Pedigree Group Limited, used
under licence in this publication.

£7.99

RIVAL DESTINIES...

Are you ready to join Ash and Pikachu as they journey ever deeper into the fascinating Unova region? Our heroes are set to encounter intrigue, excitement and all manner of thrilling new Pokémon species! Some are friendly, some are fearsome, but all are equipped with unique skills and characteristics to keep even the most knowledgeable Trainer on their toes.

Ash's senses need to be alert at all times – it's not just new Pokémon that he needs to watch out for. As he travels from Gym to Gym, a host of new rivals are sure to present themselves! After setting out from Nuvema Town, Ash has built up an enviable collection of Gym badges, but adding to his collection may be harder than it looks. How will our hero fare against Elesa the elegant Nimbasa City Gym Leader, or indeed Alder the Champion of Unova?

Against such awesome opposition, it's lucky that Ash and Pikachu aren't alone in their quest. His friends Iris and Cilan are there every step of the way, but pal Bianca and rival Trip also pop in un-expected places! These Trainers face their own trials too – one needs to fight for the right to continue her travels while another has to confront a returning challenge from the past – and the gang must team up to save an island from the clashing forces of three powerful and mysterious Pokémon!

RD Health Warning:
Ash better watch his back in Unova – Team Rocket are still trying to track the Trainer down and steal his Pikachu! Jessie, James, Meowth and their evil crime organisation are determined to wreak havoc wherever they go.

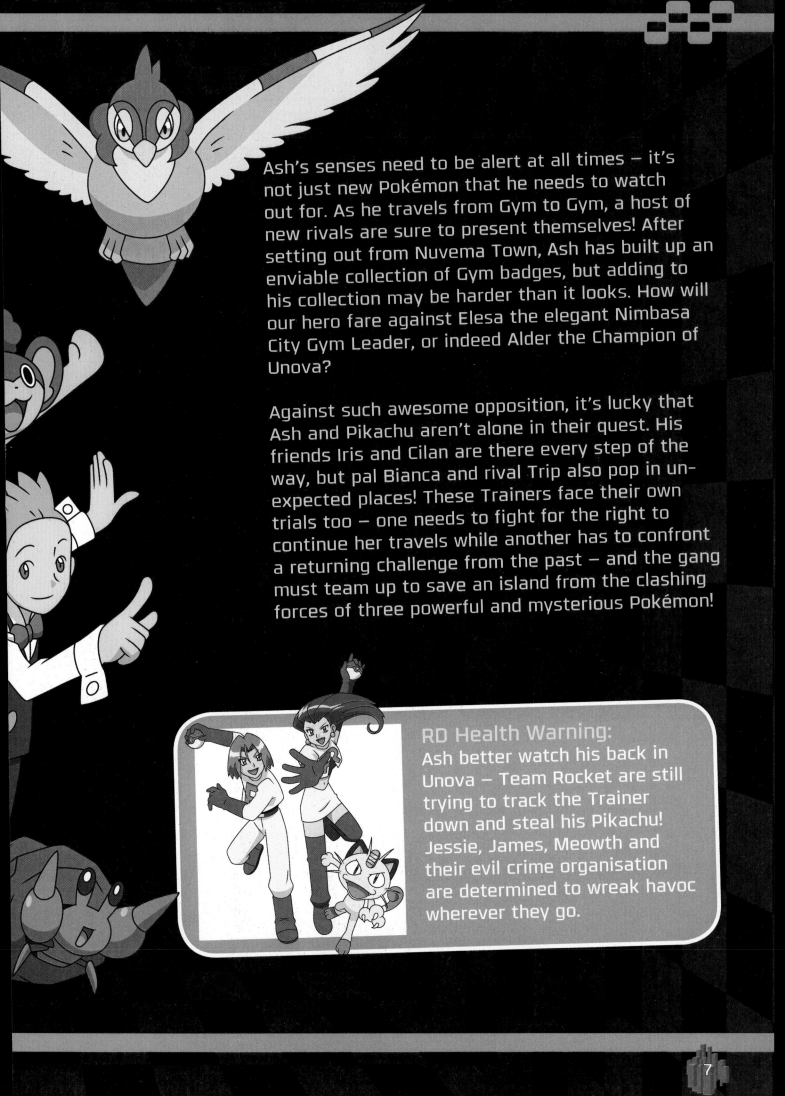

RD ROLL CALL ASH AND PIKACHU

We've come along way with our hero Ash Ketchum, but there's still so many adventures out there waiting to be shared! Ever since he first left his home in Pallet Town, Ash has been obsessed with one goal – becoming a great Pokémon Master. From those early days in Kanto, Ash's quest has taken him through many regions, collecting Gym badges whenever and wherever he can. His faithful best pal Pikachu has been there to support him through good times and bad.

Although they didn't get along at first, Ash and Pikachu are now utterly inseparable. As well as treasured memories, the pair share the same unstinting loyalty, deep courage and feisty personalities! Pikachu is also the rare Pokémon that doesn't travel in a Poké Ball, choosing to ride on Ash's shoulder instead. Ash doesn't mind – he likes it that way!

Ash and Pikachu don't know what dangers and delights still await them in the Unova region, but they are determined to make the most of every experience. Ash uses his breathtaking duels in the Gym to improve his Pokémon knowledge. The young Trainer won't give up until he's earned a clutch of Gym badges and entered the Unova League tournament!

CHECK OUT THE AWESOME POKÉMON JOINING ASH ON HIS UNOVA JOURNEY!

SNIVY

Type: Grass
Profile: A calm and intelligent Pokémon that increases in velocity when exposed to sunlight. It can photosynthesize when it bathes its tail in solar rays.

TEPIG

Type: Fire
Profile: Tepig can blast fireballs from its nostrils to repel attackers. It also uses this ability to roast berries before eating them. If the Pokémon catches a cold, it blows out black smoke.

OSHAWOTT

Type: Water
Profile: This Water-type has a hard, detachable scalchop set within its chest, made from the same material as claws. In combat, Oshawott detaches the scalchop and hurls it at its foes.

SCRAGGY

Type: Dark-Fighting
Profile: Scraggy has an exceptionally thick skull that its uses to headbutt anyone that makes eye contact with it. When under attack, it pulls its rubbery skin up to shield its neck.

TRANQUILL

Type: Normal-Flying
Profile: This Pokémon has an exceptional homing instinct, enabling it to return to its Trainer no matter what distance or obstacles may separate them. Wild Tranquill live in deep forest.

SWADLOON

Type: Bug-Grass
Profile: Swadloon keeps warm by wrapping itself in leaves. This Pokémon has a nurturing effect on the forests it inhabits, turning the falling leaves around it into fertilizing nutrients.

PALPITOAD

Type: Water-Ground
Profile: This amphibious species can create water waves or ground tremors by vibrating the bumps on its head. It has a long, sticky tongue that it uses to snare prey.

ROGGENROLA

Type: Rock
Profile: A Pokémon with a hexagonal ear and an internal energy core. Roggenrola was first discovered a hundred years ago in an earthquake fissure. Its body is as hard as steel.

RD ROLL CALL
IRIS

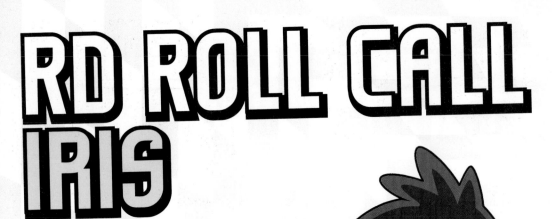

Ash's journey has taken all sorts of twists and turns since he met up with Iris! His feisty travel companion comes from a village that specializes in raising Dragon-type Pokémon. When the Trainer first spied Iris, she was picking berries from a bush, causing Ash to mistake her thick hair for an exotic new Pokémon species!

Iris has got lots to learn, but when it comes to Pokémon, she's confident and focused. She is also passionate about fulfilling her dream of becoming a Dragon Master. Iris is devoted to her Axew. When it gets frightened, the Pokémon hides in her hair.

Iris may be young, but she's already hooked up with some amazing Pokémon!

AXEW

Type: Dragon
Profile: Axew relies heavily on its sharp tusks. It uses them to mark out territory and crush food. If a tusk breaks, a replacement begins to grow very quickly.

EXCADRILL

Type: Ground-Steel
Profile: This Pokémon is equipped with a steel drill, strong enough to bore through iron plates. Excadrill dwells in maze-like nests deep underground. It is an expert tunneller.

EMOLGA

Type: Electric-Flying
Profile: This tree-top dwelling Pokémon makes electricity in its cheeks, storing the charge in its cape-like membrane. It also uses the membrane to fly, releasing power as it glides.

RD ROLL CALL CILAN

Cilan is a new friend, but he's already irreplaceable. After being defeated by Ash in the Striaton City Gym, Cilan decided to join the young Trainer on his journey through Unova.

Although Cilan is a Gym Leader along with his brothers Chili and Cress, he is also a Pokémon Connoisseur. He uses this expertise to size up the compatibility between Trainers and their Pokémon then give advice on how they might get along better. As well as being a reliable buddy, Cilan has all sorts of other, hidden talents – from cracking mysteries to cooking up delicious meals. Ash wouldn't go anywhere without him!

The pick of the Pokédex
Cilan has a trio of trusty to Pokémon to support him in battle.

PANSAGE

Type: Grass
Profile: The edible leaf on Pansage's head has stress-relieving properties. The Grass-type is happy to share the leaf with any weary-looking Pokémon it meets. It lives in forests.

DWEBBLE

Type: Bug-Rock
Profile: Dwebble secretes a liquid from its mouth so powerful it can melt rocks. It selects a rock to make its home, but quickly moves on to another one if it gets damaged or broken.

STUNFISK

Type: Ground-Electric
Profile: A Pokémon with a tough outer skin that can withstand enormous pressure. Stunfisk hides in the mud along seashores, surprising its prey with a sharp jolt of electricity.

RD ROLL CALL
BIANCA

Bianca doesn't travel everywhere with Ash and Pikachu— she's a free spirit following her own quest through the Unova region. The young Trainer is sometimes flaky and unpredictable, but she feels honoured to count our heroes as her friends.

The crew first met Bianca when she was trying to capture a Minccino with her Pignite. Not of all her dealings with Pokémon go so well, but she has good intentions to prove to her father that she has got what it takes to be up there with the best! Bianca doesn't mean to be messy and forgetful – it just happens sometimes!

The pick of the Pokédex
Bianca has worked hard to capture her personal Pokémon team!

PIGNITE

Type: Fire-Fighting
Profile: Anything that Pignite consumes becomes fuel for the fire in its stomach. The flames burn hotter when the Pokémon gets angry, sharpening the speed and power of its movement.

MINCCINO

Type: Normal
Profile: A Pokémon that thrives in a neat and tidy habitat, Minccino uses its broom-like tail to sweep constantly. When it encounters another Minccino, the pair rub their tails together in greeting.

SHELMET

Type: Bug
Profile: Shelmet protects itself from attack by shutting the lid of its shell. For reasons as yet unknown, it evolves when both it and Karrablast are bathed in electric-like energy.

RD ROLL CALL
TRIP

Ash's rival Trip only recently began his journey as a Pokémon Trainer, but he has big ambitions. Trip is determined to become the ultimate Pokémon champion! Ash and Trip have been adversaries from the very beginning, doing everything they can to show the other that they have superior skills in the battle arena.

Trip has been dreaming of glory ever since the day he met Alder the Unova League Champion. Alder advised Trip to battle often and grow strong – a motto that the young Trainer has taken to heart. Does Trip have what it takes to make it all the way to the top? Only time will tell!

The pick of the Pokédex
Study these members of Trip's team – who knows when you might encounter these species in battle?

TRANQUILL
[Tr]ip often battles with a [Tr]anquill, just like his arch-[ri]val Ash Ketchum! Trip's [Tr]anquill is incredibly fast.

SERVINE

Type: Grass
Profile: Servine glides along the ground as if it is sliding. If it is being stalked, the Pokémon eludes attackers by slipping unseen into the undergrowth. Its Vine Whip is extremely effective.

FRILLISH

Type: Water-Ghost
Profile: A Pokémon that lives five miles below the surface of the ocean, Frillish paralyses victims with its poison and then drags them down to its lair. It has thin, veil-like arms.

LAMPENT

Type: Ghost-Fire
Profile: People live in fear of this Pokémon, which scours cities searching for the spirits of the fallen. Lampent is actually capable of stealing the spirit out of a body should it choose to do so.

WATCH YOUR BACK!

Some of Unova's Fighting types are hard to rival for speed, skill and sheer strength! How well do you know the fascinating species that roam across this region? Follow each clue chain, and then try to name the Pokémon hinted at below. Budding Trainers should aim for three out of three!

1. A small but mighty Pokémon that walks on two legs	2. An elegant fighter with razor-sharp claws	3. Known as the Karate Pokémon

Helps out on construction sites	Uses concentration to add speed and focus to its moves	Psyches itself up by tying its belt

Carries a squared-off log under its arm	Weighs in at 20.0 kg	Trains for many hours on isolated mountain
	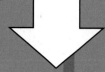	
Evolves into Gurdurr	Evolves into Mienshao	Has no evolutions
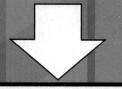		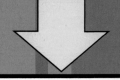
_____	_____	_____

Finding it tough? Use the Unova Pokédex on page 36 to help you! If you're really struggling, you'll find the answers at the back of the book.

TITANS OF UNOVA

Snivy, Tepig and Oshawott may not appear intimidating, but look what they can evolve into! Samurott has a lethal sword built into its body armour, Serperior halts opponents just by rearing its head and Emboar can hurl fire punches by setting its own fists alight!

It's up to you to put this awesome Pokémon scene back together again. Grab a pen, then draw a line to match the right jigsaw pieces to the gaps in the big picture.

3 pieces below are correct and 3 are not, can you find out which is which?

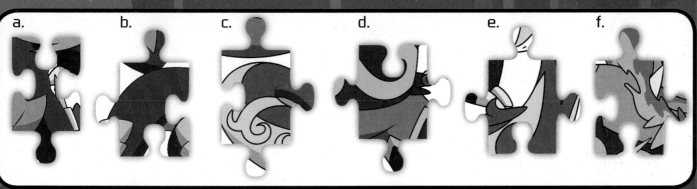

a.   b.   c.   d.   e.   f.

EVOLUTION REVOLUTIONS

This disk has been inscribed with eight knock-out Pokémon and their Evolutions. It would make a handy ready reference for a new Trainer, if Team Rocket hadn't crept in and rotated the inner circles. Now nothing is lined up correctly and none of the Evolutions make sense!

Ash needs you to unpick this mess. Study the inner circles and try and spot how far out of line each one has been turned. When you're ready, write the correct Evolutions at the bottom of the opposite page.

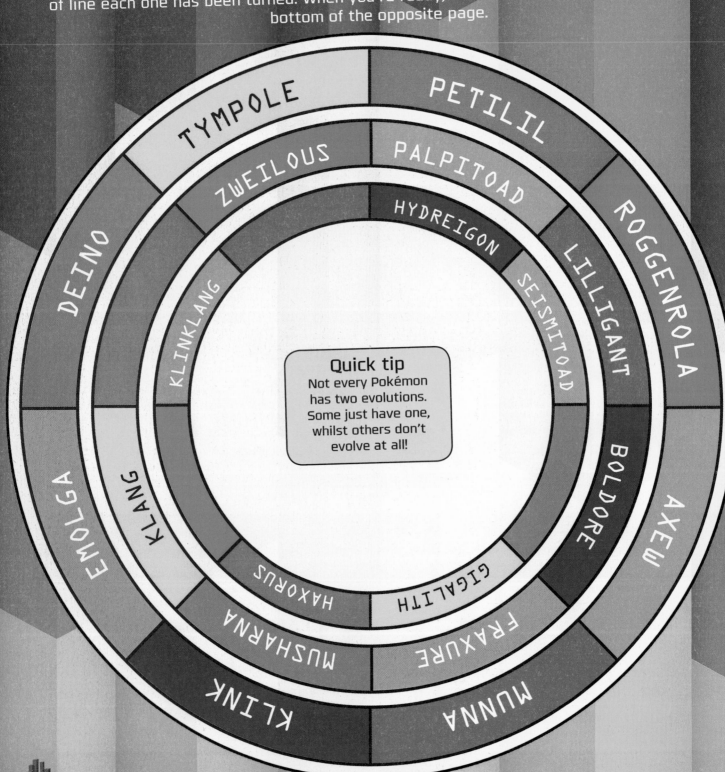

TYMPOLE

PETILIL

ZWEILOUS

PALPITOAD

DEINO

HYDREIGON

ROGGENROLA

SEISMITOAD

LILLIGANT

KLINKLANG

Quick tip
Not every Pokémon has two evolutions. Some just have one, whilst others don't evolve at all!

BOLDORE

EMOLGA

KLANG

AXEW

HAXORUS

GIGALITH

MUSHARNA

FRAXURE

KLINK

MUNNA

1. PETILIL

....

....

2. ROGGENROLA

....
....

3. AXEW

....
....

4. MUNNA

....
....

5. KLINK

....

....

6. EMOLGA

....
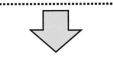
....

7. DEINO

....
....

8. TYMPOLE

....

....

CILAN'S CONNOISSEUR QUIZ

Did you know that Cilan is an A-class Pokémon Connoisseur? Ash's clever pal specializes in identifying the compatibility between Trainers and their Pokémon, a skill that requires an insightful mind and years of experience. Pokémon Connoisseurs often help new Unova Trainers pick their best battle companions.

There are four classes of Pokémon Connoisseur – C, B, A and S. Cilan dreams of one-day reaching S level! How would you rate as a Connoisseur? Use this tick test to find out!

1. Bianca has a Shelmet. What is its most effective move?

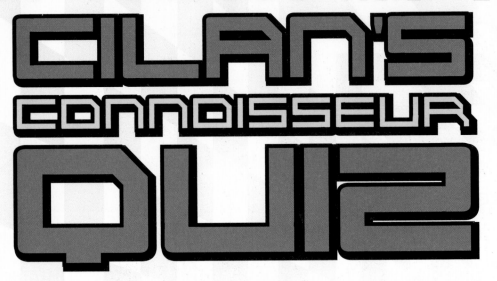

a. Volt Charge

b. Double Kick

c. Acid

2. What makes Team Rocket's Meowth so unusual?

a. It can speak like a human

b. It can detect Pikachu using sensors in its whiskers

c. It has poison fangs

3. What does Ash's Scraggy have a reputation for doing?

a. Head-butting everyone it meets ☐

b. Sleeping for hours on end ☐

c. Running at tremendous speed ☐

4. Iris dreams of becoming a Dragon Master. What is her most loyal Dragon-type Pokémon?

a. Excadrill ☐

b. Emolga ☐

c. Axew ☐

5. Nimbasa City Gym Leader Elesa battles with a formidable Zebstrika. What happens when her Pokémon gets angry?

a. It starts to kick and buck ☐

b. Lightning shoots from its mane ☐

c. Stamping make the ground rumble ☐

6. Trip believes that Trainers need strength to make it to the top. Which of these mighty Pokémon are loyal to him?

a. Servine ☐

b. Mandibuzz ☐

c. Carracosta ☐

7. Which of these species is not one of the three Unova Starter Pokémon?

a. Tepig
b. Snivy
c. Minccino

□
□
□

8. Officer Jenny chooses to work with a Herdier. Why?

a. They are fearless in battle □
b. They are always loyal and obedient to their Trainers □
c. They are happy to travel on Officer Jenny's motorbike □

9. Unova League Champion Alder is close with his Bouffalant. What is its species name?

a. Bash Buffalo
b. Stampeder
c. Headbutt Buffalo

□
□
□

10. What do both Alder and Ash think the secret is of good battling?

a. Hours of practise
b. People and Pokémon working in harmony
c. Finding obedient Pokémon to battle with

How did you do?

0-2 – C-class
You're on the very start of your journey as a Connoisseur. Keep practicing!

3-5 – B-class
A promising score, but there is much more for you to learn in Unova.

6-8 – A-class
Excellent observation – you're building a deep knowledge of Pokémon and their behaviour.

9-10 – S-class
Congratulations. You have what it takes to become a true Pokémon Connoisseur!

ENTER ELESA, ELECTRIFYING GYM LEADER!

Ash and his friends have arrived at Nimbasa City, ready to begin the Trainer's fourth Gym Badge challenge. As they stand back to admire the impressive Gym, the last thing they expect to run into is an old friend...

Ash rubbed his eyes. Could that really be Bianca standing in front of him?
The girl grinned.

"I came to Nimbasa City to have a Gym Battle," she nodded. "I even made an appointment!"

Ash scowled at Pikachu. They hadn't come all this way for Bianca to mess up their plans! Bianca tried to push past Ash, but the Trainer blocked her path.

"I got to the Gym first!" he argued. Bianca refused to listen, but Cilan stepped in to break things up.

"Just relax," he told the pair. "I suggest you leave it up to the Gym Leader."

"Who is the Nimbasa City Gym Leader anyway?" asked Iris.

That was easy! Bianca pulled a glossy magazine out of her satchel. She pointed to a stunning supermodel posing elegantly on the front cover.

"That's Elesa," she explained, "everyone's crazy about her!"
Iris squealed with delight. "She's gorgeous!"

The gang hurried up the Gym steps, desperate to catch a glimpse of its resident superstar. But instead of meeting Elesa, there was just a note taped to the door.

"'I regret that I'll be away for the Fashion Show'," read Cilan.

Bianca flicked through her magazine, certain that she had read something about this.

"Here it is!" she cried, flicking to the right page. "Elesa's appearing in her very own fashion show. It's only close by."

Bianca giggled with excitement – a fashion show sounded totally glamorous!

"What about you?" asked Iris, turning to Ash. Ash shrugged.

"Without a Gym Leader I guess I am stuck," he frowned.

Cilan spotted an opportunity. If they went to the Fashion Show too, Ash might be able to learn about Elesa before they got to battle. "You're right," agreed Ash. "Let's go!"

The Nimbasa Fashion Show was just as glamorous as Bianca had said it would be. Thousands of people stood side by side in a swish auditorium in the heart of the city centre. Fans cheered as Elesa strutted up and down the catwalk in a series of amazing outfits.

"She's so elegant!" cooed Iris. "Incredible!" agreed Bianca.

The friends suddenly gasped – Elesa was walking towards them! The Gym Leader jumped down from the runway and picked her way through the crowds. Instead of rushing up to say hi to the girls, Elesa had her eyes fixed on Ash's Pikachu!

"I'm tingling all over!" she cried. "I've never seen a Pikachu up close. You shine like the sun!"

Ash and Bianca both tried to explain that they were here to challenge Elesa to a battle. Luckily the Gym Leader seemed happy to oblige.

"I'll meet you all at the Gym after the fashion show," she smiled.

The friends made their way to the Gym's entrance hall.

"What's that?" asked Ash, pointing to a sleek red carriage waiting in a bay in front of them.

"I would imagine that we ride this to get to the battlefield," replied Cilan.

Bianca jumped in and pulled down the safety bar. She had read about this monorail in her guidebook!

As soon as everybody else was in, the carriage leapt forward. "Aaaahhh!"

The monorail zipped along the track at high speed. The passengers were forced to cling on as it veered left and right, while below dazzled in a blaze of multi-coloured neon lights.

"It's the ultimate Electric-type Gym," announced Iris.

"Beautiful!" chipped in Bianca.

The ride was so much fun Ash and Bianca almost forgot about their upcoming Gym battles, but when the monorail stopped Elesa was there to greet them. The pair's determination instantly came rushing back.

"Welcome to the Nimbasa City Gym," called Elesa, leading her guests into a bright hallway. Bianca took a step forward.

"I have an appointment to challenge you to a battle!" she announced boldly.

Ash kicked the ground. Why hadn't he had the sense to book an appointment, too?

"First things first," said Elesa, leading Bianca towards a set of double doors. "There's someone waiting to see you."

When the doors rolled open, Bianca was in for a surprise. There was her father, smiling and waving at her!

"I've come to bring you home," explained Bianca's dad. "I think might have been too hasty allowing you to go off on this journey."

Bianca shook her head. She couldn't go home – it was her dream to stay here until she made it into the Unova League!

"I'm not going to quit," she insisted. "You don't have to give up on your dream," reasoned her father, "but a journey can be a dangerous thing."

Elesa's eyes twinkled. She suggested holding a Gym battle to show Bianca's dad just how much his little girl had already grown during her time on the road.

Bianca's dad thought for a moment, then looked his daughter in the eye.

"If you lose to Elesa do you promise that you'll come home with me?" he asked.

"All right!" nodded Bianca.
Ash and his friends swapped uneasy looks – battling a Gym Leader was going to be tough!

"What if you lose?" asked Iris.
"I guess I just won't," Bianca replied.

Ash, Cilan and Iris followed Bianca through a chrome walkway. On the other side, crowds of spectators whooped and cheered. The place was electric!

"This is the Nimbasa City Gym arena," Elesa declared proudly. "A battle isn't just about battling. It's a way for Trainers to express themselves."

The judge called the challengers to their places. She explained that the battle would only be over when three Pokémon on either side were unable to continue.

Elesa hurled her Poké Ball into the battlefield.

"Zebstrika," she called, "the bright light's on you!"

Undeterred, Bianca brought out a small, grey Shelmet.

SHELMET

THE SNAIL POKÉMON

SHELMET CAN SPIT A STICKY, POISONOUS ACID WHEN ATTACKING, AND IT CAN DEFEND ITSELF BY CLOSING ITS SHELL.

Bianca decided to play to Shelmet's strengths, kicking the combat off with the Pokémon's famous Acid move. Shelmet's attack was fast, but unfortunately Zebstrika was even faster.

"Zebstrika's speed is dizzying, right?" remarked Elesa.

The Gym Leader's Pokémon plunged into a ground-shattering Flame Charge. Despite Shelmet's brave efforts to counter its rival, Zebstrika soon had the advantage. Ash winced as Shelmut was sent spinning into the air with a merciless Double Kick.

"No!" cried Bianca.

Too late. Shelmet was unable to battle.

"Zebstrika wins it," confirmed the judge.

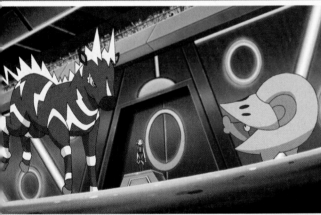

23

Bianca recalled Shelmet to its Poké Ball. She had been defeated in the first round, but the plucky Trainer was not ready to give up just yet.

"Your turn Minccino, let's go!"
Ash and his friends watched nervously as the second Pokémon took its place in the battle arena.

"I wonder how Minccino will deal with Zebstrika's speed?" whispered Cilan.

"Use DoubleSlap!" shouted Bianca, her eyes focused on Elesa's Pokémon.

Minccino lashed its tail against Zebstrika, following it up with an impressive barrage from its Swift attacks. For a moment its rival was forced onto the defensive, but the situation didn't last. Ash and his pals cringed as Zebstrika prepared for the counterattack.

"Use Flame Charge!" yelled Elesa.
Zebstrika pounded its hooves on the ground, surrounding itself in a red-hot ball of flame. Minccino was blasted backwards at a terrifying speed.

"Use Hyper Voice," urged Bianca desperately. Minccino tried its best, but it was out of resources. Elesa returned with another awesome Flame Charge that knocked the weakened Pokémon to the dirt. The crowd gasped as Zebstrika unleashed a final Double Kick. Minccino's fight was over.

"Minccino is unable to battle," confirmed the judge. "Zebstrika is the winner!"
Ash and Iris shook their heads. Bianca was giving it her best shot, but Elesa was just too strong. Now she only had one more chance.

"I have to win this!" muttered Bianca, summoning her final Pokémon. "Pignite... it's all yours!"

Pignite stood firmly in the battle arena. Bianca was counting on its strength to dominate Zebstrika.

"Let's go!" ordered Bianca. "Use Flamethrower!"

Ash watched intently as Pignite summoned up a blast of heat so intense, the Gym was lit up with coloured flame. Zebstrika responded with Double Kick, but for now it seemed to have met its match. Pignite dodged the counterattack just in the nick of time.

"Use Flame Charge!" commanded Elesa, sending Zebstrika in one more time. Bianca responded with a mighty Heat Crash.

The rivals watched in awe as the titans clashed above their heads.

"Your Pignite is very strong," Elesa said in admiration. "It gives me a charge!"

Unfortunately Pignite's dominance wasn't to last. There was a huge explosion as Zebstrika used Flame Charge to knock Pignite to the ground.

"Time for the final act," announced Elesa, sending Zebstrika back in with its signature Wild Charge move.

Ash and his friends covered their eyes as the Pokémon locked together in a ball of white light. When the smoke had cleared, Pignite was motionless on the floor.

"Pignite is unable to battle," said the judge. "Gym Leader Elesa wins the match!"

The crowd went wild, but Bianca looked devastated.
"That means that she has to go home with her father," sighed Cilan.
Ash nodded. "Guess so..."

Bianca's dad was waiting for her outside the Nimbasa Gym.

"You battled well," he said, "but we made a deal."

Bianca didn't answer – she needed to see how Shelmet was doing first! The friends gathered round the battle-weary Pokémon. Taking on Zebstrika had been a massive challenge.

"This should make Shelmet feel a whole lot better," soothed Iris, bending down to give the Pokémon a nutritious drink.

"Thank you," Bianca smiled sadly.

"Before you go, let's head to the Pokémon Center," suggested Elesa. "Zebstrika could also use some tender loving care."

After the gang had checked in with Nurse Joy, Cilan decided to rustle up a bite to eat for everyone. Perhaps if the friends could sit down and talk with Bianca's dad, they could persuade him to let his daughter continue her Unova journey.

"These are the best sandwiches ever!" cried Iris, tucking into the feast. Bianca and her dad agreed.

Ash spotted his opportunity to talk to his rival's father. Despite trying every argument that he could think of, nothing seemed to work.

"I'm not opposed to Bianca going on a journey in the future," he explained, "but she needs to learn better judgement first." Ash only had one more trick up his sleeve – he challenged Bianca's father to a Pokémon battle. If he won, Bianca would be allowed to stay on her journey.

Bianca's dad thought it over. He had been a Trainer too in his younger days.

"I'll accept your challenge, if you promise me one thing..." he replied. "If you lose you have to promise to go back to your home – Pallet Town!"

The stakes were giddily high, but what could Ash do? The battle was on!

"I'll volunteer to be the judge," said Elesa.

Ash and Bianca's dad stood face to face in the battle arena.

"You've got a lot of courage to challenge me to a Pokémon battle," said Bianca's father, suddenly swirling a red cloak around his body. "When I was a young man, I was called the 'Red Meteor'!"

Cilan stared at the girls in astonishment.

"Your dad has a different side to him Bianca!" gasped Iris.

Bianca nodded. "Yeah, and that different side loves to battle!"

There was no time to find out more, the Red Meteor had already called out a fierce Darmanitan! Ash tried hard to keep his cool.

"Do you want to battle too?" he asked his Oshawott.

The Water-type jumped up and down, spinning the scalchop on its chest.

"All right," confirmed Elesa, "let battle begin!"

The fight was fast and furious right from the very start.

"Now Darmanitan," instructed Bianca's dad, "Flamethrower!"

The awesome Pokémon launched into a blistering attack, but Oshawott was ready. It countered the move with a huge jet of water, then consolidated with Tackle! Bianca's dad laughed, relishing the challenge.

"Intercept it with Fire Punch!" he shouted, forcing Oshawott backwards.

Cilan was impressed. Bianca's dad clearly loved it bold and spicy!

"Maybe too spicy," winced Iris.

Ash had no intention of giving up … not now or ever! Oshawott picked itself up, going back in hard with a Shell Blade attack. Bianca's dad tried to counter with a Fire Punch, but Ash had already launch his Pokémon into a perfectly-timed Aqua Jet.

"It worked!" cheered Iris.

Maybe Ash really could win this thing!

"Your Oshawott is quite impressive," conceded Bianca's dad, "but the stronger the opponent, the more my Red Flash rises to the challenge." As if drawing on a newfound hidden strength, Darmanitan pounded its enemy with a merciless Fire Punch and Flame Charge attack. Ash had to admit it, now his Pokémon seemed the weaker of the two!

Bianca had seen enough.

"Stop already!" she begged. "If you lose this battle Ash, you're going to have to go back to Pallet Town. I'll give up and go back home with Dad like I said!"

Ash refused to budge. Bianca was their friend – he wouldn't walk out on her when she needed him most! Although she didn't travel everywhere with them, the gang had shared a ton of special times.

"We've camped out and watched the twinkling stars together," explained Iris. Cilan agreed.

"We've even drunk from the same waterfall," added Iris.

Bianca was totally touched. As far as Ash and his pals saw it, she was their buddy and that was that!

"All right," chuckled her father, "what do you say that we finish this Ash?"

Ash replied with a forceful Aqua Jet.

"Darmanitan!" ordered Bianca's dad. "Use Flare Blitz!"

Iris and Bianca covered their eyes as the two Pokémon went at each other with maximum force. The Gym shook and rumbled as fire and water collided. Oshawott put up a mighty resistance, but it couldn't hold on – the shattered Pokémon collapsed on its back.

"Oshawott is unable to battle!" announced Elesa. "Darmanitan is the winner!"

Bianca gasped. It had been a bold challenge, but Ash had been defeated. The young Trainer was devastated.

"Since Ash has lost, is he going back to Pallet Town?" asked Iris, her face pink with concern.

The Red Meteor recalled his Darmanitan, then paused for a moment.

Bianca's dad helped Ash back to his feet.

"It is true that journeys are filled with danger, but after battling with Ash I can remember the good times, too!" he grinned. "I want you to get stronger on your journey Bianca. And with Ash and all of his friends you will!"

Bianca blinked. Was her dad really giving his permission for her to carry on?

"Daddy!" she cried, rushing up to give him a hug. "I will get stronger."

"That's my girl," he smiled proudly. Ash, Iris and Cilan beamed from ear-to-ear – the battle had been worthwhile after all.

"That is wonderful," agreed Elesa, thrilled for her visitor.

Bianca didn't stop to chat – she was already scooting out of the Nimbasa Gym.

"I'm on my way to the Desert Resort!" she exclaimed. "See you later!"

"You can see why I was worried. She's always like that," shrugged Bianca's father. Iris pointed to a green satchel slung down in the corner.

"Isn't that Bianca's bag?" Ash's opponent scooped it up and bolted after his wayward daughter.

"Hold on!" his voice echoed behind him. "You forgot your bag!"

The friends couldn't help but laugh. When would they bump into Bianca next? Whenever it happened, it was sure to be interesting!

"So Bianca stays on her journey," said Cilan.

"And Ash, too!" piped up Iris.

Ash punched the air, but Elesa still had one more surprise for the Trainer.

"You did come for a battle," she reminded him. "I'll see you tomorrow at the Gym!"

"OK!" cheered Ash, hugging and high-fiving Pikachu. "And then I'm going to get me my next Gym badge!"

Bianca's journey continues, thanks to our heroes. As for Ash, his nail-biting battle with Elesa is only a good night's sleep away!

POKÉMON

PICTURE WORDSEARCH

Unova abounds with eye-boggling Pokémon, ranging from the tame to the totally, terrifyingly wild. There are ten fascinating species hiding in this word grid, but before you can find them you've got to name them! Study the picture clues, then use the Pokédex on page 36 to help you identify each one. Next try and locate all 10 Pokémon in the wordsearch square below.

1 _____

2 _____

3 _____

4 _____

5 _____

6 _____

7 _____

8 _____

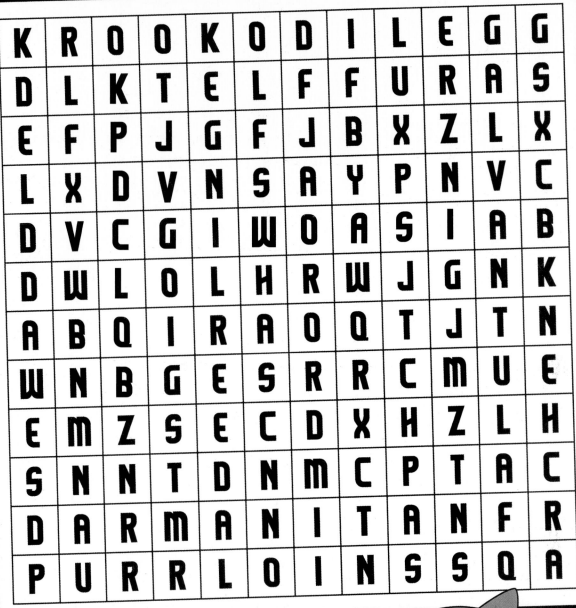

K	R	O	O	K	O	D	I	L	E	G	G
D	L	K	T	E	L	F	F	U	R	A	S
E	F	P	J	G	F	J	B	X	Z	L	X
L	X	D	V	N	S	A	Y	P	N	V	C
D	V	C	G	I	W	O	A	S	I	A	B
D	W	L	O	L	H	R	W	J	G	N	K
A	B	Q	I	R	A	O	Q	T	J	T	N
W	N	B	G	E	S	R	R	C	M	U	E
E	M	Z	S	E	C	D	X	H	Z	L	H
S	N	N	T	D	N	M	C	P	T	A	C
D	A	R	M	A	N	I	T	A	N	F	R
P	U	R	R	L	O	I	N	S	S	Q	A

9

10

_____ _____

31

ASH VS TRIP
TRAINER TEST PART I
ASH'S CHALLENGE

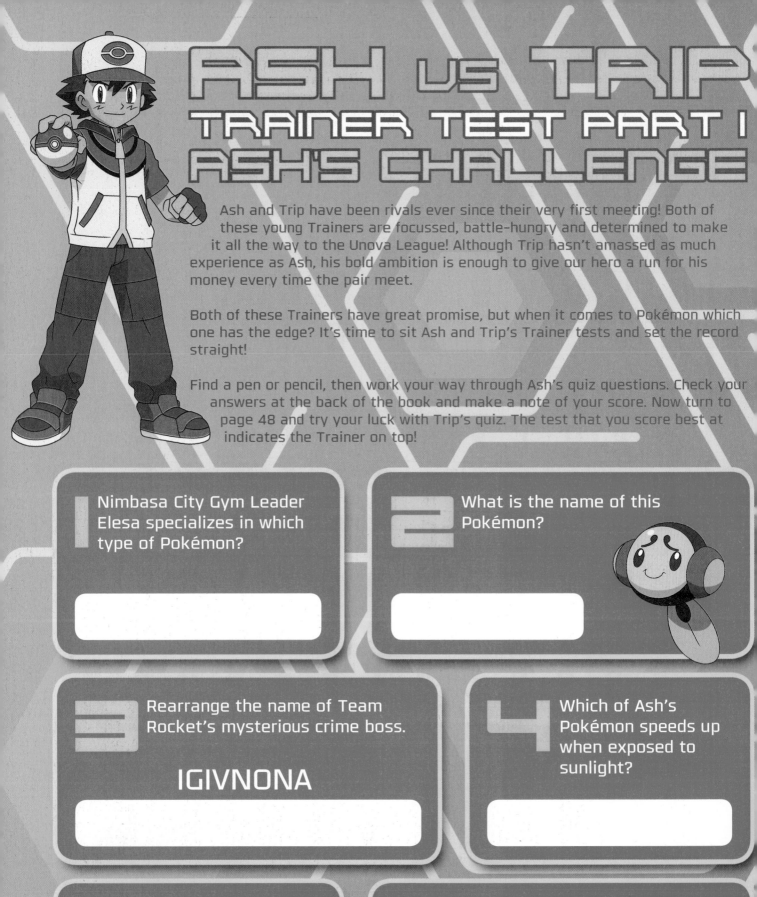

Ash and Trip have been rivals ever since their very first meeting! Both of these young Trainers are focussed, battle-hungry and determined to make it all the way to the Unova League! Although Trip hasn't amassed as much experience as Ash, his bold ambition is enough to give our hero a run for his money every time the pair meet.

Both of these Trainers have great promise, but when it comes to Pokémon which one has the edge? It's time to sit Ash and Trip's Trainer tests and set the record straight!

Find a pen or pencil, then work your way through Ash's quiz questions. Check your answers at the back of the book and make a note of your score. Now turn to page 48 and try your luck with Trip's quiz. The test that you score best at indicates the Trainer on top!

1 Nimbasa City Gym Leader Elesa specializes in which type of Pokémon?

2 What is the name of this Pokémon?

3 Rearrange the name of Team Rocket's mysterious crime boss.

IGIVNONA

4 Which of Ash's Pokémon speeds up when exposed to sunlight?

5 Which Unova city can be entered via a modern drawbridge?

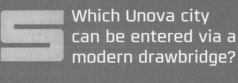

6 What is Swadloon's final evolution?

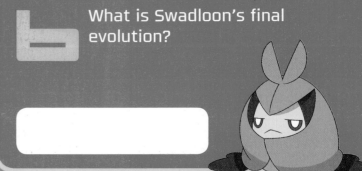

7 Reshiram is one of Unova's mighty Pokémon. What is the name of the other?

8 Who runs the research lab in Nuvema Town?

9 Which of these Pokémon commonly flocks in cities?

10 What gadget is every Trainer's must-have ready reference tool?

11 What Pokémon wraps itself in leaves to keep away the cold?

12 What does a Pokémon breeder specialize in?

13 Which of these Pokémon did not evolve?

15 Name this Pokémon.

14 What establishments do Don Georges own all across Unova?

POKéMON PLACE MAT

Cilan believes that eating well is the recipe for success for all Pokémon Trainers. Food keeps us strong and healthy, plus it's good for the mind, too! The clever Connoisseur has presented a cool Pokémon place mat for you to make and personalize.

What are you waiting for? In just a few minutes, you could become a meal-time Pokémon Master!

For each Pokémon placemat, you will need:
• Tracing paper
• Pencil
• Ruler
• Thin white card
• Felt-tip pens
• Black fine-tipped pen
• Sticky back plastic
• Scissors

1. Lay a sheet of tracing paper over the design on the facing page. Carefully trace over the design in pencil, using a ruler to help get the edges straight.

2. When you've copied the place mat design exactly, place the tracing sheet on a rectangle of thin card. Carefully transfer the design onto the card by drawing over it one more time.

3. Take away the tracing paper and colour in the place mat in your favourite Pokémon shades. Don't forget to write your name in the centre so that everyone knows it's yours!

4. Turn the place mat over and draw on some bright patterns to decorate the reverse.

Why not draw in some of your favourite Pokémon or a portrait of yourself?

5. When you've filled your place mat with colour on both sides, take a fine-tipped black pen and draw around the edges of the characters and shapes. This will give your pictures amazing definition.

6. Unroll a tube of sticky back plastic and peel off the backing paper. Give your place mat a shake to make sure that it is completely clean, then lay it onto the plastic. Carefully smooth off any bubbles or creases and cut off the roll. Now turn the mat over and cover the other side.

7. Neatly trim the edges so that all the excess plastic is removed. Your place mat is ready to use!

ULTIMATE UNOVA POKÉDEX

Ash would be lost in the Unova region without his trusty Pokédex! The state of the art gadget is crammed with facts and stats about the local Pokémon species. The young Trainer can look up and learn about Pokémon types, behaviour and Evolutions.

Here's your chance to sneak a peek over Ash's shoulder! This bumper section features the latest Pokédex entries on some of the region's most fascinating species. Read the pages carefully, remembering as much as you can. Keep expanding your Pokémon knowledge and one day you could be winning Unova Gym badges too!

ACCELGOR

Type:
Bug
Category:
Shell Out
Height:
0.8m
Weight:
25.3kg

ALOMOMOLA

Type:
Water
Category:
Caring
Height:
1.2m
Weight:
31.6kg

AMOONGUSS

Type:
Grass-Poison
Category:
Mushroom
Height:
0.6m
Weight:
10.5kg

ARCHEN

Type:
Rock-Flying
Category:
First Bird
Height:
0.5m
Weight:
9.5kg

ARCHEOPS

Type:
Rock-Flying
Category:
First Bird
Height:
1.4m
Weight:
32.0kg

AUDINO

Type:
Normal
Category:
Hearing
Height:
1.1m
Weight:
31.0kg

AXEW

Type:
Dragon
Category:
Tusk
Height:
0.6m
Weight:
18.0kg

BASCULIN

Type:
Water
Category:
Hostile
Height:
1.0m
Weight:
18.0g

BEARTIC

Type:
Ice
Category:
Freezing
Height:
2.6m
Weight:
260.0kg

BEHEEYEM

Type:
Psychic
Category:
Cerebral
Height:
1.0m
Weight:
34.5kg

BISHARP

Type:
Dark-Steel
Category:
Sword Blade
Height:
1.6m
Weight:
70.0kg

BLITZLE

Type:
Electric
Category:
Electrified
Height:
0.8m
Weight:
29.8kg

BOLDORE
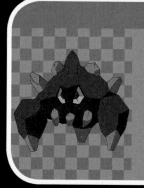
Type:
Rock
Category:
Ore
Height:
0.9m
Weight:
102.0kg

BOUFFALANT

Type:
Normal
Category:
Bash Buffalo
Height:
1.6m
Weight:
94.6kg

BRAVIARY

Type:
Normal-Flying
Category
Valiant
Height:
1.5m
Weight:
41.0kg

CARRACOSTA

Type:
Water-Rock
Category:
Prototurtle
Height:
1.2m
Weight:
81.0kg

CHANDELURE
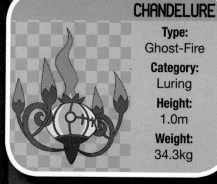
Type:
Ghost-Fire
Category:
Luring
Height:
1.0m
Weight:
34.3kg

CINCCINO

Type:
Normal
Category:
Scarf
Height:
0.5m
Weight:
7.5kg

COBALION

Type:
Steel-Fighting
Category:
Iron Will
Height:
2.1m
Weight:
250.0kg

COFAGRIGUS

Type:
Ghost
Category:
Coffin
Height:
1.7m
Weight:
76.5kg

CONKELDURR

Type:
Fighting
Category:
Muscular
Height:
1.4m
Weight:
87.0kg

COTTONEE

Type:
Grass
Category:
Cotton Puff
Height:
0.3m
Weight:
0.6kg

CRUSTLE

Type:
Bug-Rock
Category:
Stone Home
Height:
1.4m
Weight:
200.0kg

CRYOGONAL

Type:
Ice
Category:
Crystallizing
Height:
1.1m
Weight:
148.0kg

CUBCHOO

Type:
Ice
Category:
Chill
Height:
0.5m
Weight:
8.5kg

DARMANITAN

Type:
Fire
Category:
Blazing
Height:
1.3m
Weight:
92.9kg

DARUMAKA

Type:
Fire
Category:
Zen Charm
Height:
0.6m
Weight:
37.5kg

DEERLING

Type:
Normal-Grass
Category:
Season
Height:
0.6m
Weight:
19.5kg

DEINO

Type:
Dark-Dragon
Category:
Irate
Height:
0.8m
Weight:
17.3kg

DEWOTT

Type:
Water
Category:
Discipline
Height:
0.8m
Weight:
24.5kg

DRILBUR

Type:
Ground
Category:
Mole
Height:
0.3m
Weight:
8.5kg

DRUDDIGON

Type:
Dragon
Category:
Cave
Height:
1.6m
Weight:
139.0kg

DUCKLETT

Type:
Water-Flying
Category:
Water Bird
Height:
0.5m
Weight:
5.5kg

DUOSION

Type:
Psychic
Category:
Mitosis
Height:
0.6m
Weight:
8.0kg

DURANT
Type:
Bug-Steel
Category:
Iron Ant
Height:
0.3m
Weight:
33.0kg

DWEBBLE
Type:
Bug-Rock
Category:
Rock Inn
Height:
0.3m
Weight:
14.5kg

EELEKTRIK
Type:
Electric
Category:
EleFish
Height:
1.2m
Weight:
22.0kg

EELEKTROSS
Type:
Electric
Category:
EleFish
Height:
2.1m
Weight:
80.5kg

ELGYEM
Type:
Psychic
Category:
Cerebral
Height:
0.5m
Weight:
9.0kg

EMBOAR

Type:
Fire-Fighting
Category:
Mega Fire Pig
Height:
1.6m
Weight:
150.0kg

EMOLGA

Type:
Electric-Flying
Category:
Sky Squirrel
Height:
0.4m
Weight:
5.0kg

ESCAVALIER

Type:
Bug-Steel
Category:
Cavalry
Height:
1.0m
Weight:
33.0kg

EXCADRILL

Type:
Ground-Steel
Category:
Subterrene
Height:
0.7m
Weight:
40.4kg

FERROSEED

Type:
Grass-Steel
Category:
Thorn Seed
Height:
0.6m
Weight:
18.8kg

FERROTHORN

Type:
Grass-Steel
Category:
Thorn Pod
Height:
1.0m
Weight:
110.0kg

FOONGUS

Type:
Grass-Poison
Category:
Mushroom
Height:
0.2m
Weight:
1.0kg

FRAXURE
Type:
Dragon
Category:
Axe Jaw
Height:
1.0m
Weight:
36.0kg

FRILLISH
Type:
Water-Ghost
Category:
Floating
Height:
1.2m
Weight:
33.0kg

GALVANTULA
Type:
Bug-Electric
Category:
EleSpider
Height:
0.8m
Weight:
14.3kg

GARBODOR

Type:
Poison
Category:
Trash Heap
Height:
1.9m
Weight:
107.3kg

GIGALITH

Type:
Rock
Category:
Compressed
Height:
1.7m
Weight:
260.0kg

GOLETT
Type:
Ground-Ghost
Category:
Automaton
Height:
1.0m
Weight:
92.0kg

GOLURK

Type:
Ground-Ghost
Category:
Automaton
Height:
2.8m
Weight:
330.0kg

GOTHITA

Type:
Psychic
Category:
Fixation
Height:
0.4m
Weight:
5.8kg

GOTHITELLE
Type:
Psychic
Category:
Astral Body
Height:
1.5m
Weight:
44.0kg

GOTHORITA

Type:
Psychic

Category:
Manipulate

Height:
0.7m

Weight:
18.0kg

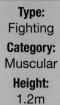

GURDURR

Type:
Fighting

Category:
Muscular

Height:
1.2m

Weight:
40.0kg

HAXORUS

Type:
Dragon

Category:
Axe Jaw

Height:
1.8m

Weight:
105.5kg

HEATMOR

Type:
Fire

Category:
Anteater

Height:
1.4m

Weight:
58.0kg

HERDIER

Type:
Normal

Category:
Loyal Dog

Height:
0.9m

Weight:
14.7kg

HYDREIGON

Type:
Dark-Dragon

Category:
Brutal

Height:
1.8m

Weight:
160.0kg

JELLICENT

Type:
Water-Ghost

Category:
Floating

Height:
2.2m

Weight:
135.0kg

JOLTIK

Type:
Bug-Electric

Category:
Attaching

Height:
0.1m

Weight:
0.6kg

KARRABLAST

Type:
Bug

Category:
Clamping

Height:
0.5m

Weight:
5.9kg

KLANG

Type:
Steel

Category:
Gear

Height:
0.6m

Weight:
51.0kg

KLINK

Type:
Steel

Category:
Gear

Height:
0.3m

Weight:
21.0kg

KLINGKLANG

Type:
Steel

Category:
Gear

Height:
0.6m

Weight:
81.0kg

KROKOROK

Type:
Ground-Dark

Category:
Desert Croc

Height:
1.0m

Weight:
33.4kg

KROOKODILE

Type:
Ground-Dark

Category:
Intimidation

Height:
1.5m

Weight:
96.3kg

KYUREM

Type:
Dragon-Ice

Category:
Boundary

Height:
3.0m

Weight:
325.0kg

LAMPENT

Type:
Ghost-Fire
Category:
Lamp
Height:
0.6m
Weight:
13.0kg

LANDORUS

Type:
Ground-Flying
Category:
Abundance
Height:
1.5m
Weight:
68.0kg

LARVESTA

Type:
Bug-Fire
Category:
Torch
Height:
1.1m
Weight:
28.8kg

LEAVANNY

Type:
Bug-Grass
Category:
Nurturing
Height:
1.2m
Weight:
20.5kg

LIEPARD
Type:
Dark
Category:
Cruel
Height:
1.1m
Weight:
37.5kg

LILLIGANT

Type:
Grass
Category:
Flowering
Height:
1.1m
Weight:
16.3kg

LILLIPUP

Type:
Normal
Category:
Puppy
Height:
0.4m
Weight:
4.1kg

LITWICK

Type:
Ghost-Fire
Category:
Candle
Height:
0.3m
Weight:
3.1kg

MANDIBUZZ

Type:
Dark-Flying
Category:
Bone Vulture
Height:
1.2m
Weight:
39.5kg

MARACTUS

Type:
Grass
Category:
Cactus
Height:
1.0m
Weight:
28.0kg

MIENFOO

Type:
Fighting
Category:
Martial Arts
Height:
0.9m
Weight:
20.0kg

MIENSHAO

Type:
Fighting
Category:
Martial Arts
Height:
1.4m
Weight:
35.5kg

MINCCINO

Type:
Normal
Category:
Chinchilla
Height:
0.4m
Weight:
5.8kg

MUNNA

Type:
Psychic
Category:
Dream Eater
Height:
0.6m
Weight:
23.3kg

MUSHARNA

Type:
Psychic
Category:
Drowsing
Height:
1.1m
Weight:
60.5kg

OSHAWOTT

Type:
Water
Category:
Sea Otter
Height:
0.5m
Weight:
5.9kg

PALPITOAD
Type:
Water-Ground
Category:
Vibration
Height:
0.8m
Weight:
17.0kg

PANPOUR

Type:
Water
Category:
Spray
Height:
0.6m
Weight:
13.5kg

PANSAGE

Type:
Grass
Category:
Grass Monkey
Height:
0.6m
Weight:
10.5kg

PANSEAR

Type:
Fire
Category:
High Temp
Height:
0.6m
Weight:
11.0kg

PATRAT

Type:
Normal
Category:
Scout
Height:
0.5m
Weight:
11.6kg

PAWNIARD

Type:
Dark-Steel
Category:
Sharp Blade
Height:
0.5m
Weight:
10.2kg

PETILIL

Type:
Grass
Category:
Bulb
Height:
0.5m
Weight:
6.6kg

PIDOVE
Type:
Tiny Pigeon
Category:
Normal-Flying
Height:
0.3m
Weight:
2.1kg

PIGNITE

Type:
Fire-Fighting
Category:
Fire Pig
Height:
1.0m
Weight:
55.5kg

PURRLOIN

Type:
Dark
Category:
Devious
Height:
0.4m
Weight:
10.1kg

RESHIRAM

Type:
Dragon-Fire
Category:
Vast White
Height:
3.2m
Weight:
330.0kg

REUNICLUS

Type:
Psychic
Category:
Multiplying
Height:
1.0m
Weight:
20.1kg

ROGGENROLA

Type:
Rock
Category:
Mantle
Height:
0.4m
Weight:
18.0kg

RUFFLET

Type:
Normal-Flying
Category:
Eaglet
Height:
0.5m
Weight:
10.5kg

SAMUROTT
Type:
Water
Category:
Formidable
Height:
1.5m
Weight:
94.6kg

SANDILE
Type:
Ground-Dark
Category:
Desert Croc
Height:
0.7m
Weight:
15.2kg

SAWK
Type:
Fighting
Category:
Karate
Height:
1.4m
Weight:
51.0kg

SAWSBUCK
Type:
Normal-Grass
Category:
Season
Height:
1.9m
Weight:
92.5kg

SCOLIPEDE
Type:
Bug-Poison
Category:
Megapede
Height:
2.5m
Weight:
200.5kg

SCRAFTY
Type:
Dark-Flying
Category:
Hoodlum
Height:
1.1m
Weight:
30.0kg

SCRAGGY
Type:
Dark-Fighting
Category:
Shedding
Height:
0.6m
Weight:
11.8kg

SEISMITOAD
Type:
Water-Ground
Category:
Vibration
Height:
1.5m
Weight:
62.0kg

SERPERIOR
Type:
Grass
Category:
Regal
Height:
3.3m
Weight:
63.0kg

SERVINE
Type:
Grass
Category:
Grass Snake
Height:
0.8m
Weight:
16.0kg

SEWADDLE
Type:
Bug-Grass
Category:
Sewing
Height:
0.3m
Weight:
2.5kg

SHELMET
Type:
Bug
Category:
Snail
Height:
0.4m
Weight:
7.7kg

SIGILYPH
Type:
Psychic-Flying
Category:
Avianoid
Height:
1.4m
Weight:
14.0kg

SIMIPOUR
Type:
Water
Category:
Geyser
Height:
1.0m
Weight:
29.0kg

SIMISAGE
Type:
Grass
Category:
Thorn Monkey
Height:
1.1m
Weight:
30.5kg

SIMISEAR

Type:
Fire
Category:
Ember
Height:
1.0m
Weight:
28.0kg

SNIVY
Type:
Grass
Category:
Grass Snake
Height:
0.6m
Weight:
8.1kg

SOLOSIS

Type:
Psychic
Category:
Cell
Height:
0.3m
Weight:
1.0kg

STOUTLAND

Type:
Normal
Category:
Big-Hearted
Height:
1.2m
Weight:
61.0kg

STUNFISK

Type:
Ground-Electric
Category:
Trap
Height:
0.7m
Weight:
11.0kg

SWADLOON

Type:
Bug-Grass
Category:
Leaf-Wrapped
Height:
0.5m
Weight:
7.3kg

SWANNA

Type:
Water-Flying
Category:
White Bird
Height:
1.3m
Weight:
24.2kg

SWOOBAT

Type:
Psychic-Flying
Category:
Courting
Height:
0.9m
Weight:
10.5kg

TEPIG

Type:
Fire
Category:
Fire Pig
Height:
0.5m
Weight:
9.9kg

TERRAKION

Type:
Rock-Fighting
Category:
Cavern
Height:
1.9m
Weight:
260.0kg

THROH

Type:
Fighting
Category:
Judo
Height:
1.3m
Weight:
55.5kg

THUNDURUS

Type:
Electric-Flying
Category:
Bolt Strike
Height:
1.5m
Weight:
61.0kg

TIMBURR

Type:
Fighting
Category:
Muscular
Height:
0.6m
Weight:
12.5kg

TIRTOUGA
Type:
Water-Rock
Category:
Prototurtle
Height:
0.7m
Weight:
16.5kg

TORNADUS

Type:
Flying
Category:
Cyclone
Height:
1.5m
Weight:
63.0kg

TRANQUILL

Type:
Normal-Flying
Category:
Wild Pigeon
Height:
0.6m
Weight:
15.0kg

TRUBBISH

Type:
Poison
Category:
Trash Bag
Height:
0.6m
Weight:
31.0kg

TYMPOLE

Type:
Water
Category:
Tadpole
Height:
0.5m
Weight:
4.5kg

TYNAMO

Type:
Electric
Category:
EleFish
Height:
0.2m
Weight:
0.3kg

UNFEZANT

Type:
Normal-Flying
Category:
Proud
Height:
1.2m
Weight:
29.0kg

VANILLISH

Type:
Ice
Category:
Icy Snow
Height:
1.1m
Weight:
41.0kg

VANILLITE

Type:
Ice
Category:
Fresh Snow
Height:
0.4m
Weight:
5.7kg

VANILLUXE

Type:
Ice
Category:
Snowstorm
Height:
1.3m
Weight:
57.5kg

VENIPEDE

Type:
Bug-Poison
Category:
Centipede
Height:
0.4m
Weight:
5.3kg

VICTINI

Type:
Psychic-Fire
Category:
Victory
Height:
0.4m
Weight:
4.0kg

VIRIZON

Type:
Grass-Fighting
Category:
Grassland
Height:
2.0m
Weight:
200.0kg

VOLCARONA

Type:
Bug-Fire
Category:
Sun
Height:
1.6m
Weight:
46.0kg

VULLABY

Type:
Dark-Flying
Category:
Diapered
Height:
0.5m
Weight:
9.0kg

WATCHOG

Type:
Normal
Category:
Lookout
Height:
1.1m
Weight:
27.0kg

WHIMSICOTT

Type:
Grass
Category:
Windveiled
Height:
0.7m
Weight:
6.6kg

WHIRLIPEDE

Type:
Bug-Poison
Category:
Curlipede
Height:
1.2m
Weight:
58.5kg

WOOBAT

Type:
Psychic-Flying
Category:
Bat
Height:
0.4m
Weight:
2.1kg

YAMASK

Type:
Ghost
Category:
Spirit
Height:
0.5m
Weight:
1.5kg

ZEBSTRIKA

Type:
Electric
Category:
Thunderbolt
Height:
1.6m
Weight:
79.5kg

ZEKROM

Type:
Dragon-Electric
Category:
Deep Black
Height:
2.9m
Weight:
345.0kg

ZOROROARK

Type:
Dark
Category:
Illusion Fox
Height:
1.6m
Weight:
81.1kg

ZORUA

Type:
Dark
Category:
Tricky Fox
Height:
0.7m
Weight:
12.5kg

ZWEILOUS

Type:
Dark-Dragon
Category:
Hostile
Height:
1.4m
Weight:
50.0kg

ULTIMATE
UNOVA POKÉDEX

NIMBASA CITY MAZE

Ash and his friends are on a race against time to get to the Nimbasa City Gym! The Trainer needs to challenge Elesa to a Gym battle before she takes on any more rivals. By night Nimbasa becomes a dazzling network of neon signs and bright lights – not an easy place to see clearly.

Put your pen or pencil on the START, then trace a route through the city lights, all the way to Elesa's door.

ASH vs TRIP
TRAINER TEST PART II
ASH'S CHALLENGE

Now it's Trip's turn to test your mettle! Ash's rival has lined up a super-tough test for wannabe Trainers to take on. Try and answer every question, turning to the Pokédex pages if you need a little extra help. When you're finished compare your score to the mark you notched up for Ash's quiz on page 32. The test with the highest total will reveal the sharpest Trainer in town for today at least!

Team Ash
Ash can be hot-headed and reckless, but he's also determined to do right by the Pokémon he meets. This Trainer is caring, loyal and kind.

Team Trip
At times Trip comes across as grumpy and serious, but no one can doubt his commitment to achieving his goals. Trip is dedicated, brave and clever.

Find out what happened when Ash met Trip in the story on page 64!

1 Name the person behind the desk in every Pokémon Center.

2 What unevolved Pokémon can blow fire from its nose?

3 What type of Pokémon is Vanillite?

4 What is this Pokémon's next Evolution?

5 Which City Gym is Cilan leader of, alongside his two brothers?

6 Which of Ash's Pokémon has a detachable scalchop on its belly?

7 Nacrene City is also known as the City of Engineering. True or False?

8 Which Pokémon has plants on its horns that change with the seasons?

9 Identify this Pokémon.

10 A Trainer needs eight of these to enter the Unova League?

11 Which Ice-type turns to steam if its body temperature rises too high?

12 Who is the Champion of the Unova League?

13 Name this Pokémon.

14 What type of Pokémon is Cofagrigus?

15 Which of these Pokémon can live on water or on land?

DAZZLING IN THE NIMBASA GYM!

Having arrived in Nimbasa City, Ash is now mulling over strategies for his upcoming Gym battle against Gym Leader Elesa, as the rest of our heroes look on. Can Ash come up with a plan to win his fourth Unova Gym badge?

Iris and Cilan stood together in a corner, talking in hushed voices. Neither friend wanted to disturb Ash's preparations for his next Gym battle!

"He's been like that for quite a while…" whispered Iris, pointing across to the Trainer. Cilan nodded. Ash and Pikachu had been poring over their notebooks ever since they'd arrived at the Nimbasa City Gym. It wasn't the heroes' normal pre-battle routine, but a well thought-out strategy had to help their chances of defeating Elesa.

"Let's see, Pikachu," mused Ash. "Since Elesa's Zebstrika uses Electric-type moves, an Electric-type like you won't be affected."

"Pika-Pika!" agreed the loyal Pokémon. Suddenly Ash shook his head. If Pikachu wasn't affected it meant that Zebstrika wouldn't feel the impact of any of its Electric-type moves either!

"You know what?" decided Ash. "I want to try using my other Pokémon."

Pikachu folded its arms sadly. If there was going to be some action in the arena, he wanted to be a part of it!

Ash refused to budge. The way he saw it, he had been relying on Pikachu, Tepig, Oshawott and a couple of other Pokémon for a while now. It was time to give a new species a try.

"That's the one!" announced the Trainer,

suddenly scribbling a name into his book. Ash went to call Professor Juniper using one of the Pokémon Center's communication monitors mounted on the wall beside him. Within seconds, Professor Juniper appeared on the screen.

"Great to see you!" she smiled, pleased to see that the Trainer was working hard to earn another Unova Gym badge.

"Elesa has a seriously powerful Electric-type," explained Ash. "So I'd like to switch one of my Pokémon with you."
Professor Juniper agreed at once.

"It's as good as done. Which one would like to switch?"
Pikachu was startled. It didn't like the way this new strategy of Ash's was shaping up!

The next day, the visitors were ready to ride the monorail into the battle arena.

"All right!" whooped Ash, as the carriage whisked him and his friends through the bright lights of Nimbasa City.
Before the battle could begin the determined Trainer had one last matter to attend to.

"Would you guys mind holding onto Pikachu for me?" he asked, setting the disappointed Electric-type onto the ground.

"Are you sure?" questioned Cilan.
Ash replied with a firm nod. "Pikachu's not going to battle this time."

"No problem," smiled Iris, holding out her arms.
"We'll cheer for you as a group!" added Cilan.
Ash took a deep breath, then walked towards the imposing entrance of the Nimbasa Gym. The doors slid apart to reveal an enormous high tech battle arena, packed with cheering girls. A dazzling spotlight suddenly lit up in the centre of the chamber.

"I've been waiting for you!" called Elesa, stepping out of the darkness.
As soon as they heard the Gym Leader speak, the crowds began to shout even louder.

"Hi!" replied Ash. "Thanks for accepting

Elesa turned to address her adoring fans. Girls squealed and screamed in anticipation, desperate to see their Gym Leader's latest show of skill. Iris, Cilan, Pikachu and Axew took their places on the sidelines.

"Prepare for a battle that glistens!" promised Elesa. "I'll be shining as bright as the sun!"
The judge signalled for the crowd to become silent.

"The Nimbasa Gym battle will now begin!" she announced. "This will be a three-on-three match and the battle will be over when all three Pokémon on either side are unable to continue. Only the challenger may substitute Pokémon."
Iris looked thoughtfully at Ash.

"I wonder what kind of strategy he's settled on?" she mused.
Cilan was wondering the same thing. Ash only had a moment to recap on his plan of attack – the battle was ready to be played out!

The crowds went wild as Elesa threw her first Poké Ball into the arena.

"Feel the spark! And feel the tingle!" she sang, "watch me mix and mingle!"
Just as Ash and his friends had predicted, the bright lights were on Zebstrika again! The awesome Pokémon marched into position, scraping its hoof in anticipation of the duel ahead.

"Elesa beat all of Bianca's Pokémon using just Zebstrika," remembered Iris, starting to feel nervous for her friend.

"Such a powerful Electric-type," agreed Cilan. Only Ash didn't seem phased by his opponent. He was ready to roll with his secret strategy!

"Palpitoad!" he called, "I choose you!"
Elesa nodded in appreciation as the Trainer's blue Pokémon appeared. It wasn't a dazzling

strategy, but Ash was clearly using his head. As a Ground-type, Zebstrika's Electric-type moves wouldn't have any effect on Palpitoad.

"Flame Charge!" ordered Elesa. Zebstrika morphed into a ball of flame, but the attack was soon repelled.

"Palpitoad's also a Water-type," cheered Iris, "so Fire-type moves aren't very effective."

Instead of trying something new, Elesa sent her Pokémon into another forceful Flame Charge move.

Cilan looked on appreciatively. This was no accident – Zebstrika's speed was increasing with every new attack! Palpitoad tried to respond with Hydro Pump, but Elesa's Pokémon used a fearsome Double Kick to send its foe tumbling across the arena.

"It appears that I've dazzled Palpitoad," concluded Elesa. "I know that it is a tough and resilient Pokémon, but how tough can it be in that state?"
Iris and Cilan looked on nervously. Ash's Pokémon was lying flat-out on the ground! Ash clenched his fists – he wasn't going to

give up that easily!

"Palpitoad," he urged. "Up!"
The brave little Pokémon slowly and deliberately struggled back to its feet. Palpitoad's battle was still on!

It was a brilliant comeback.

"All right!" whistled Ash, signalling for Palpitoad to reply with a blistering Supersonic.

"Zebstrika," cried Elesa. "No!"
The Gym Leader's cries were helpless. Elesa was confused and disorientated! Ash saw his chance, quickly pummelling Zebstrika with a forceful Mud Shot and Hydro Pump attack. Palpitoad's water blast sent its rival slamming into the Battle arena's metal doors.

"Zebstrika is unable to battle," confirmed the judge. "Palpitoad wins!"
Elesa held her Poké Ball out so Zebstrika could return.

"You went down with grace," she said, smiling gently. "You're beautiful even when covered in mud."

Palpitoad had been an inspired choice. Zebstrika was powerful, but Elesa couldn't use her Wild Charge attack because of the type Ash had selected.

"If it ain't broke, don't fix it," decided the young Trainer, refusing the option of swapping in another Pokémon. "Full speed ahead."
Cilan winced. He wasn't so sure that his friend had made the right call this time!

"I fear that Palpitoad is gradually accumulating damage," he explained to Iris. "Frankly, I'm worried."
Across the other side of the Gym, Elesa was weighing up her options very carefully.

"Ash is sparkling so much it's difficult to look, but he'll soon be spinning instead of sparkling!" she concluded. "Emolga, I choose YOU!"
Iris braced herself for another epic clash. Emolga was an Electric- and Flying-type. Within seconds, the feisty Pokémon was tumbling into a dizzying Acrobatics attack.

"Now," chucked Elesa, "Attract!"

Emolga's Attract was powerful. Hearts swirled around Palpitoad, enchanted by its rival.

"Snap out of it," begged Ash, desperate not to lose his advantage.

"I told you I'd dazzle you two, didn't I?" grinned Elesa. "Don't you see? Emolga can use other types of moves than just Electric-types! Emolga, Aerial Ace!"

Palpitoad was dispatched within moments. Iris, Cilan and their Pokémon watched in dismay as their new hope was knocked to the floor.

"Palpitoad is unable to battle!" shouted the judge. "Emolga is the winner!"

Ash rubbed his eyes in disbelief. He'd been planning on winning every battle with Palpitoad. What was he going to do now?

"You need to bring out your next Pokémon," pressed the judge. "Otherwise I'll have to disqualify you."

"Give me a few minutes, Elesa," blushed Ash, desperately trying to buy some time. Elesa chuckled mischievously.

"You didn't by chance bring just Palpitoad did you?" she asked.

Ash decided not to answer her.

The crowds waited impatiently while the challenger considered his options. A few minutes' later, Ash was ready to run back into the arena.

"Battle restart," called the judge.
'Snivy!" shouted the Trainer, tossing his Poké Ball into the field of play. "I choose you!"
The Grass-type got ready to do its worst.

"Emolga!" cooed Elesa. "Attract, won't you?"
Ash couldn't wait for Emolga to turn his Snivy's head. He countered with his own Attract move.

"An Attract battle?" gasped Cilan.
Iris dropped her head. "Isn't Snivy a girl?"
What was Ash up to? There was no way that Attract would work on another female Pokémon!

Snivy's Attract move was futile.

"Does your Snivy happen to be a female?" called Elesa.

Ash clutched his head. He'd totally forgotten about that.

"How many times will it take for Ash to learn that Attract doesn't work between girls?" wailed Iris.

Cilan looks on resigned. "This is Ash, after all…"

"So who cares?" bellowed Ash, picking himself back up again. "Electric-type moves aren't very effective on Grass-type Pokémon."

Elesa chuckled to herself. The young Trainer had forgotten another very important point.

"Emolga may be an Electric-type," she reminded him, "but remember that it's a Flying-type as well!"

"Oh man!" gulped Ash. Any Trainer worth their salt knew that Flying-type moves were super-effective on Grass-type Pokémon and Snivy was a Grass-type!

It was time for a snap decision. Ash sent Snivy in with Vine Whip before Emolga could land another attack.

The stunned crowd watched as Snivy bombarded Emolga with Leaf Blade and then Leaf Storm. Elesa's protégé was surrounded in a blur of swirling foliage, whipping round and round at devastating speed.

"Did it work?" asked Ash, when the leaves finally began to clear.

"Emolga!"

The attack was bold, but not bold enough. Emolga emerged untouched and ready for revenge.

"Now it's time to show Ash how brilliantly you can shine!" beamed Elesa. "Use Acrobatics!"

Emolga began to pummel Snivy from a great height, weakening its enemy with every blow.

"This recipe's starting to go sour," groaned Cilan.

Iris could hardly bear to watch. Emolga nearly had Snivy at its mercy!

Pikachu fizzed and sparked with rage. Seeing its best friend in trouble was enough to make it short circuit!

"Watching Ash battle can whip you into a froth, huh?" said Cilan.

Snivy was still standing, but only just.

"Your Pokémon is obviously quite tough," declared Elesa, "but it's time for a dazzling finish. Use Aerial Ace!"

Emolga thundered towards Snivy at astonishing speed, scoring a direct hit. Iris and Cilan watched in dismay as Snivy collapsed onto the sand. Ash was in trouble again!

"Snivy is unable to battle!" announced the judge. "Emolga wins!"

The crowds cheered and screamed, delighted by their Gym Leader's latest display of skill. Emolga flashed a smile at her adoring fans.

"My Emolga positively glows," she exclaimed. "I'm glad you feel the same way!"

Ash sadly brought out his Poké Ball – poor Snivy deserved a good rest. As for him? He needed to find another Pokémon to battle with... fast!

The judge was already getting impatient, but Ash had no idea what his next move should be. None of his Pokémon had an advantage over Electric and Flying-types.

"What am I gonna do?" he howled. Behind him, Pikachu nearly exploded with frustration. Here was one Pokémon ready to square up to any Emolga out there!

"You'd better hurry up," snapped the judge, "or you'll be disqualified."

The Trainer still sat dithering, panic etched across his face.

It was time for Pikachu to give Ash a helping hand. A flash of sparks lit up the arena, blasting its friend off the ground.

"Hey Pikachu," said Ash, turning to face his buddy for the first time. "Got any ideas?"

The judge tapped her foot. "Choose your next Pokémon NOW."

At last Ash saw what had been staring him in the face all along.

"I thought I needed to think up some sort of awesome plan by myself," he explained, "but I can't battle without my Pokémon. I need your help Pikachu... what do you say?"

Pikachu was already in position. All it wanted was to bring on that battle!

"Now that's the Ash that I know!" Cilan grinned. "Forget some plan. This is a recipe for success!"

Iris nodded enthusiastically. Since both Pokémon were Electric-types, this Battle would have to be decided on spirit. Elesa and Ash were charged up and ready to rock, both sending Emolga and Pikachu in with blistering Electro Ball moves. Their first combat was a dead-heat, but Ash quickly followed up with Pikachu's dominating Quick Attack. The crowd fell silent. Emolga was out of the game!

"Pikachu is the winner!" announced the judge. Elesa recalled Emolga to her Poké Ball.

"You were brilliant," she said sadly, "Like the sun."

Now it was Ash and Pikachu's turn to shine brightly. All around the battle arena, fans chattered anxiously. They had never seen Elesa so serious about a challenger before.

TYNAMO

THE ELEFISH POKÉMON

TYNAMO USUALLY LIVES IN GROUPS AND HAS AN ELECTRICITY-GENERATING ORGAN, WHICH DISCHARGES WHEN IN DISTRESS.

Iris grabbed Cilan's sleeve. The hushed whispers were making her nervous. It sounded like the crowds were expecting Elesa to bring out some sort of secret weapon. The Gym Leader did not disappoint.

"It's time for my Electric Queen," she said boldly. "The bright light is you... Tynamo!" A small white Pokémon burst into view. Ash couldn't understand it – Elesa's Tynamo didn't look intimidating at all!

"And here I was waiting for some crazy-looking Pokémon," he muttered, pulling his Pokédex out of his pocket.

Cilan urged caution – appearances could be deceptive in the b0attle arena!

"OK," agreed Ash. "I'd still better be sharp."

Elesa used her dazzling skill to unleash Tynamo's full power on its rival. Pikachu was battered again and again by the Electric-type's stunning Tackle move.

"Tynamo's got some incredible speed!" marvelled Cilan.
Iris groaned. How could Pikachu dodge these relentless attacks?

"So where's your sparkle now?" taunted Elesa, watching Pikachu getting pummelled into the ground.
Pikachu was weak and dazed, but Ash knew his pal better than that.

"I know you can keep battling," he begged. "Please Pikachu!"
Somehow the feisty little Pokémon managed to crawl back out of its hole, pulling itself back up to full height.

"I think Pikachu's all right!" cheered Iris.
Cilan wasn't able to cheer quite yet. Ash still had to work out a way of dealing with Tynamo's speed.

"Tynamo!" shouted Elesa, "use Tackle again!" Ash and Pikachu braced themselves for yet another attack. As they focused together, Trainer and Pokémon were completely in synch.

"Now what, Pikachu?" asked Ash.
It was if they could both understand what the other one was thinking! Pikachu got its message across loud and clear – the pair needed to go in with a mass of Thunderbolts! Even Elesa had to admire the sight of a Trainer and his Pokémon working as one. Ash and Pikachu had made an inspired decision together. Although Electric-type moves weren't effective on Tynamo, the confusion they created freed up the way for a stinging Iron Tail attack.

"Oh no!" screamed Elesa.
Tynamo was down and... out!

Pikachu had won the battle and the match!

"All right!" bellowed Ash, high-fiving his loyal Pokémon.

Elesa comforted her Tynamo, assuring it that the defeat wasn't its fault.

"You were as brilliantly sparkling as could be!" she smiled, walking over to congratulate her challenger.

Cilan nodded. "It was a battle with a rich and bold quality."

"You made me remember so much," Elesa continued. "A brilliant display is not the most important thing. It's that unbreakable bond between Trainer and Pokémon."

Ash gave Pikachu a wide grin.

"My buddy reminds me of that all the time," he agreed modestly.

Elesa presented the Trainer with a smart presentation case. Inside was the coveted Bolt Badge!

"Thanks!" shouted Ash, leaping into the air. "I just got number four!"

As the sun began to set, Elesa showed her new friends out of the Nimbasa Gym. It had truly been a great battle, spiced up with lots of heat.

"Where are you off to next?" asked the Gym Leader.

"I haven't decided yet," admitted Ash. "Now let's see."

Elesa suggested Driftveil City. Apparently the Gym there was quite dazzling!

"Cool!" replied Ash, ready to set off there and then.

Cilan and Iris shrugged – trust their friend to be ready to dive straight into his next adventure!

"The Driftveil Drawbridge is closed for repairs," warned Elesa. "Why don't you stay in Nimbasa City until it's all fixed?"

Ash looked at his pals and winked. After all that excitement, he figured that they could all use a hot meal and a good night's sleep.

"I bet I can eat more than you!" he teased, lifting Pikachu onto his shoulder.

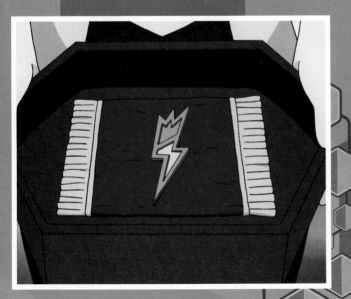

A brilliant display of teamwork has given Ash his fourth Unova Gym victory and the Bolt Badge! Now with his sights set on the Unova League, our heroes' adventure continues.

WISE WORDS

When it comes to battling Pokémon, Ash and his counterparts always have something to say! Take a close look at the six faces below, then draw a line to match each person to the correct quotation. Can you match everyone up in under a minute?

IRIS

BIANCA

TRIP

CILAN

ASH

PROF JUNIPER

A. "It's good as done! Which one would you like to switch? "

B. "I thought I needed to think up some sort of awesome plan by myself! But I forgot something... I can't battle without my Pokémon!"

C. "Now that's an exceptionally tasty strategy!"

D. "I'm staying here! I want to stay on my journey!"

E. "You had me so worried that my head was spinning and my heart racing!"

F. "My ultimate goal is getting to the Champion League – and once I get there, I'll defeat Alder!"

ROCKET RAGE

The Pokémon on this page are known for their loyalty, kindness and sensitivity – attributes that Team Rocket abhor in equal measure! Jessie, James and Meowth have decided to stir up trouble by mixing up the letters in these Pokémon names.
Can you help restore order in this annual?
Foil Team Rocket's plans by writing the correct label underneath each picture. Good luck!

1. UODANI

_ _ _ _ _ _

2. OMERBA

_ _ _ _ _ _

3. ZANUTENF

_ _ _ _ _ _ _

4. GODHCTAW

_ _ _ _ _ _ _

5. GAPSENA

_ _ _ _ _ _

6. DUTONSLAT

_ _ _ _ _ _ _

ARCHEOPS SPOT

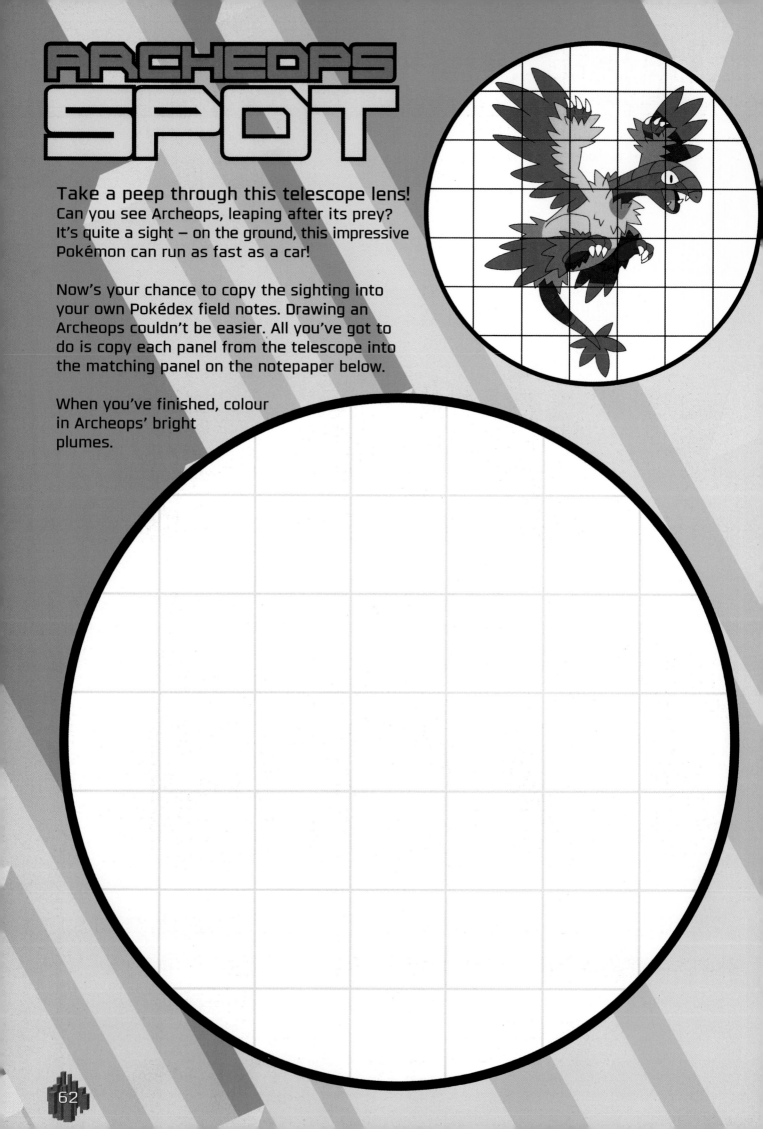

Take a peep through this telescope lens! Can you see Archeops, leaping after its prey? It's quite a sight – on the ground, this impressive Pokémon can run as fast as a car!

Now's your chance to copy the sighting into your own Pokédex field notes. Drawing an Archeops couldn't be easier. All you've got to do is copy each panel from the telescope into the matching panel on the notepaper below.

When you've finished, colour in Archeops' bright plumes.

SHADOWY SILHOUETTES

The Unova region is abundant with Dark-type Pokémon, although many take care never to stray into human sight. Can you shed some light on the shadowy forms prowling across this puzzle page? Study each silhouette, then pick a name from the list at the bottom and write it underneath the correct picture.

1.

2.

3.

4.

5.

6.

7.

8.

GOTHITELLE   MANDIBUZZ   ZWEILOUS

SCRAFTY   BISHARP   LIEPARD

PAWNIARD   PURRLOIN

63

ASH VERSUS THE CHAMPION!

Our heroes are ready to leave Nimbasa and embark on a new adventure in Driftveil City, but there's time for a little fun before they go. Ash and his friends are just starting to relax when an old rival appears to shake things up!

Cilan pointed towards a majestic red bridge, framing the horizon.

"Once we cross that drawbridge, we'll be saying farewell to Nimbasa City," he smiled sadly. Ash kept on walking, his eyes focused on the mountains in the distance. There was no time for goodbyes when another Gym battle was just round the corner! The dedicated Trainer couldn't wait to explore Driftveil and lay down his challenge in the Driftveil City Gym. Iris was just as excited... until she saw something irresistible on the other side of the road.

"Hold on guys!" she squealed, scurrying towards a pedestrian area packed with stalls, musicians and dancers.

Ash peered after his friend – the place looked totally wild! In the middle of the square an acrobat was balancing precariously on a ladder held up by a flock of trained Pidove. Nearby a group of children were giggling as they played Whack-a-Sandile with inflatable hammers.

"Whoa!" cried Ash. "It's a festival!" Cilan explained that this was actually Performer's Square – a space set aside for

street performers. Magicians, singers and artists came here from all over the Unova region.

"Awesome!" gushed Iris. "We should check it out while we're here."
Ash didn't need asking twice – he had just sniffed the amazing aromas coming from the row of food stalls lining the square.

"It all looks great," he grinned, trying to work out what to eat first. Dumplings, toffee apples, noodles – everything looked delicious! Cilan chuckled, adding, "I should have known that your stomachs would lead the way." Ash was about to order his entrée when Pikachu started chirruping loudly. The Trainer's Pokémon had spotted someone familiar – Trip!

"How's it going?" called Ash.
As soon as he heard his name Trip turned round, but he didn't smile. The old rivalry was still as strong as ever!

"Ta-daa!" shouted Ash, running up to show Trip his growing collection of Unova Gym badges. Trip didn't seem impressed at all. Instead he pulled out his own badge case and opened it up.

"One, two, three, four…" counted Ash, "Five? That's one more badge than me!"

"Of course," harrumphed Trip. "It's the difference in our skill levels. Basic stuff." Ash felt himself getting red. If this kid thought he was so special, he was going to have to prove it! He challenged Trip to a battle, but his rival dismissed the idea.

"I'm waiting for someone," he sniffed. "Alder, actually…"

"The Alder?!"
Iris, Cilan and Ash couldn't help blurting out their question. Alder was the Unova League Champion – famous all over the region for his skill at handling Pokémon.

"That's right," said Trip. "Alder's my goal, you see? Winning the Unova League is just a stepping stone as far as I'm concerned. My ultimate goal is getting to the Champion League. Once I'm there, I'll defeat Alder!" Ash's head spun. Running into Trip always gave him lots to think about!

Trip told the astonished friends that he had met Alder already. In fact, it was the champion that had set him on the path of working to become a Pokémon Trainer.

"What did Alder tell you when you met?" asked Ash, hanging on Trip's every word. Any advice from such a great man had to be worth listening to!

"He told me to battle a lot in order to become strong," replied Trip, remembering the epic meeting. He had only been a boy at the time, but he had never forgotten the wise words Alder had shared on that day. The champion had even promised to battle Trip when the time was right.

"I want to meet Alder too," said Ash. Iris sighed. It wasn't that easy. Because Alder was always travelling, no one ever knew where he was going to show up next. Suddenly a deep hearty laugh echoed round the square.

"Look!" cried Trip. "It's Alder!"

The gang spun round, desperate to catch a glimpse of the famous hero.

"Get off there! This instant!"
There indeed was Alder, trying to sweet-talk Officer Jenny! The champ had got himself comfy on her motorbike and was now trying to persuade the officer to go out on a date.

"Aww…" he grinned. "You're adorable even when you're angry."
Officer Jenny stamped her foot. She didn't care how famous Alder was, she wanted this guy off her bike right now!

"Say you'll have lunch with me," he insisted, cosying up to Officer Jenny's Herdier.
Officer Jenny held out a pair of handcuffs.
"Get off," she snapped, "or I'll put these on."
Ash gasped in surprise as Alder tumbled off the bike. Officer Jenny jumped on and revved the engine.

"Serves you right!" she shouted. "And to think you call yourself the Unova League Champion."
Alder sat on the ground, rejected and red-faced.

"Please don't go!" he called feebly, watching his crush drive into the distance.

Trip and Ash ran over and helped Alder to his feet.
"It's me!" cried Trip, smiling for the first time all day. "We only met once when I was a kid. Do you remember?"
Alder flashed the Trainer a warm grin.

"Of course I remember you," he nodded, "your name is Tristan."

"It's Trip."
"Uh, Trip, Tristan… whatever!" laughed Alder. The champ wasn't so big on details, but he didn't seem to care.
Ash couldn't hold back any longer. He introduced himself and requested a Battle there and then!

"Cool your jets!" scowled Trip. "Alder's battling me first."
Alder erupted into another one of his booming laughs. As far as he was concerned the young Trainers could both battle him – they could even do it together if they wanted!

"I want to battle you on your own," insisted Trip. "Ash can go first."
Ash looked at his rival suspiciously.
"You sure?" he asked.
"Of course," replied Trip. "You'll get creamed, so I'll get to study Alder's strength!"

Ash and Alder took their positions. Inside Ash was nervous, but he didn't flinch – the Trainer was ready to bring it on!

"So here's my Pokémon," called the champion, hurling his Poké Ball across the meadow. "Bouffalant, let's go!"

"Who's that?" wondered Ash. Before he made his selection, he decided to check his Pokédex. Ash thought carefully, then choose Pikachu.

"Hmm..." mused Cilan. "There is no type advantage when it comes to those two." Trip snorted. "I guarantee you that type advantage means nothing to a powerful Trainer like Alder!"

BOUFFALANT

THE BASH BUFFALO POKÉMON

BOUFFALANT IS POWERFUL AND DESTRUCTIVE, WILDLY CHARGING AND HEADBUTTING EVERYTHING IN ITS PATH.

Alder gave Ash the honour of making the first attack.

"Okay, you got it!" replied Ash. "Pikachu, use Thunderbolt!"
Pikachu crackled with electrical charge, delivering a blistering bolt of power onto its enemy. Bouffalant shook at the force, but stayed upright.

Ash braced himself for Alder's response... but nothing came! Instead the great man stood motionless, with his arms crossed and eyes closed.

"He's not calling any moves," gasped Iris. "You snooze, you lose!" shouted Ash, following up with a Quick Attack and then a devastating Iron Tail. The Trainer was giving it his all, but there was still zero response!

"What could Alder be thinking?" asked Iris. "I'm aware that Bouffalant's fur can absorb damage from blunt force attacks. That means that they're not having much effect," said Cilan, "but what kind of strategy is standing there and doing nothing?"

Ash and his friends waited for Alder to pull himself together.

"OK then," cried the Unova League champ, "Bouffalant! Head Charge!"

Alder's Pokémon scraped his hoof back and leapt into action. Ash gasped as the massive force of nature stampeded towards Pikachu.

"Dodge it!" he yelled, desperately.

There was no need to panic. Just before it reached Ash's Electric-type, Bouffalant turned on its heel. It had set itself a new course – straight towards its master.

"Are you mad?" yelped Alder. "Please stop being such a ch-i-l-d. Aagh!"

Too late. Bouffalant butted Trip's hero straight into a tree! There was a stunned silence as Alder slowly picked himself up again.

"An extraordinary Head Charge," conceded the champ, rubbing his head. "Oh well! I guess I lost!"

Trip stepped in. Alder couldn't give up – Bouffalant was still able to battle.

"And what about our battle?" he reminded the elder.

Alder chuckled, but shook his head. All he was up for now a good meal!

"Another time, Tristan," he replied.

"Perhaps he's waiting for Pikachu to get tired?" guessed Ash. This wasn't what he'd been expecting! "We're just going to have to keep up the attacks!"

Pikachu got ready to do his worst, battering his foe with a stinging Electro Ball.

Bouffalant lurched, then stamped its foot in frustration. Pikachu had really turned up the heat, but Alder was still doing nothing!

"I don't think Bouffalant's too happy with Alder," whispered Iris.

The massive Pokémon turned to face its master, snorting with fury.

"Perhaps Alder's champion battle style is snoring," remarked Cilan, "while standing to boot!"

Trip blinked in surprise. Cilan was right – the hero had fallen asleep! It took a nudge from Bouffalant to finally wake Alder up.

"Huh?" he spluttered. "I've been walking since yesterday, so I'm exhausted. I guess I must have dozed off."

Ash shot Pikachu a look that said, "he's got to be kidding, right?"

Trip was furious. Furious that the Unova League Champion had got his name wrong and furious that he'd been cheated out of a battle!

"Forget the battle," he glowered, "but there is one thing I want to ask you."

"All right," smiled Alder, still trying to remember the Trainer's name.

"When I was a little kid you gave me some advice that I've never forgotten," began Trip. "You said that the more I battled the stronger I'd get. If I did, I could become Champion some day! You told me that in battle, strength was the most important thing."
Alder scratched his head. He couldn't remember ever giving out that advice!

"No... no I wouldn't say strength," he concluded.

"How could you forget?" cried Trip. For years he had been turning Alder's words over and over in his head, trying to grow stronger with every new battle.

"Now let's not get stuck into the details," smiled Alder. "Let's go for something to eat Tristan. What do you say?"
Trip turned on his heel, his face screwed up with anger and disappointment. The way he saw it, this whole meeting had been a waste of time!

"I'm going to follow the path that I believe in," he shouted. "A Trainer who is strong. The only way to prove that I am right is to beat the Champion and become a winner!"

"It helps to enjoy life too," added Alder quietly.

Ash, Iris and Cilan watched Trip disappear into the distance. Although he was gone for now, the friends were sure that their paths would cross again somewhere in the Unova region.

"Look at Alder now," whispered Ash, giving Pikachu a nudge.
It seemed as though the champ had forgotten Trip already. He was spread out on the grass tickling his Bouffalant and feeding it apples. It was quite a turnaround after their epic clash earlier!

Once Bouffalant was fed, Ash and friends showed the champ to the nearest Pokémon Center.
"Nurse Joy!" cooed Alder, rushing up the counter. "You're looking radiant as always! Will you join me for dinner?"

"Come on!" urged Ash, dragging him to a table.
The gang sat down to a mouthwatering spread, but Cilan and Iris didn't have much appetite.

"It's hard to eat with an audience," explained Iris.
Alder looked behind him. The dining room was chock full of excited fans, each desperate to get their hero's autograph!

Once Alder had politely asked his fans to wait outside, there was time to eat... and talk.

"You haven't told me the purpose of your travels," smiled the Unova League Champion. Ash and his friends chattered excitedly, spilling out their most precious dreams. If they all came true one day Alder might be able to say that he ate with a Pokémon Master, a Dragon Master and a Pokémon Connoisseur! These were honourable ambitions, but Alder wondered what the youngsters had planned for after they'd achieved their goals.

"I-I've never thought about that before," shrugged Ash.

'Well," continued Alder, "what do you think you need to become a Pokémon Master?"

Ash didn't hesitate. That answer was easy!

"I must become as strong as I can!" he boomed.

"That's exactly what Trip wants," nodded Iris, "and it seems to me that they're both right. Becoming super-strong is the fastest way to become a Dragon Master, too."

"Hmm..." pondered Alder. "Are you sure it's that simple?"

Before the great man could chew the issue over, Nurse Joy burst into the room.

"This is an emergency!" she gushed. "There's a wild Gigalith on the rampage!"

Alder tore outside. In the centre of Performer's Square, a ferocious Pokémon was ripping up stalls and smashing everything in sight. Frightened people ran in every direction. Officer Jenny was trying to get things under control, but Ash didn't like the wild expression in the Gigalith's eye.

"Please stay back," warned the officer. "It's dangerous."

Suddenly the fleeing crowds noticed Alder.

"Look!" shouted one man. "The Unova League Champion will take care of this!"

Alder nodded at Officer Jenny.

"You just leave this to me," he insisted, reaching for a Poké Ball.

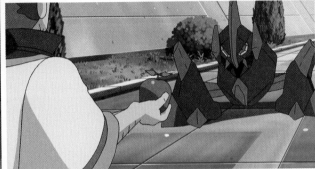

"Bouffalant, help me out," commanded Alder, before turning to the crowds. "Everybody run!"
Ash scrambled out of the way, then looked the Pokémon up.

Iris looked over her friend's shoulder and shuddered – who knew what destruction this angry Gigalith could cause?
Alder didn't seem the slightest bit phased. "Jenny," he repeated, "you better stay back too!"
Officer Jenny frowned. "But I have a job to do!"
"If I should fail, I'll leave it up to you," replied Alder, flashing his cheeky smile.
Officer Jenny took another look at the agitated Gigalith. Alder had himself a deal!

Alder took a long look at the rampaging Pokémon.
"Eat this!" he said gently, taking an apple out from under his poncho. "It will help you calm down and it tastes delicious as well." Gigalith turned a full 360. Now it was facing Alder head-on!
"Look out!" hissed Ash.
The crowds screamed as Gigalith began to pound towards the champion.
"Don't panic!" insisted Alder. "Gigalith will surely stop before it reaches me."
CCRR-AASSHH!
Alder was wrong. Ash and his pals winced as the out of control Pokémon butted the hero right into a nearby statue!
"Guess that's my cue," sighed Officer Jenny. "Herdier, use Shadow Ball!"
The officer's Pokémon squared up for the fray, but Bouffalant blocked its path.
"Good," grinned Alder. "Make sure that Herdier doesn't attack."

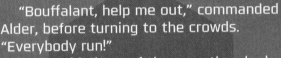

GIGALITH

THE COMPRESSED POKÉMON

GIGALITH'S ATTACKS, USING THE COMPRESSED ENERGY FROM ITS CORE, ARE POWERFULM ENOUGH TO DESTROY A MOUNTAIN.

"Has he had another blow to the head?" wondered Iris.

Alder was back on his feet and approaching Gigalith all over again!

"Now bring it!" he shouted, tackling the Pokémon head-on.

There was a titanic clash, but somehow the champion harnessed enough force to throw Gigalith back onto the ground. For a moment at least, the enormous Pokémon was trapped upside down with its feet in the air.

Ash gasped to hear Alder apologizing to his rival.

"It was easier to deal with you this way," he said gently, "so I tossed you!"

"Easier?" blurted out Ash.

Alder gave Gigalith's foot a sharp tug, pulling out a long, bent nail.

"Wouldn't you be in pain too, if this was in your foot?"

Ash, Iris and Cilan watched in awe as Alder patted and hand-fed the relieved Pokémon, explaining how the pain had caused it to lose control.

"Alder's completely transformed Gigalith," said Iris.

Ash nodded. "What an amazing guy."

"A Trainer with experience," agreed Cilan. "The savoury blend of wisdom and common sense."

Unfortunately Officer Jenny didn't share the friends' opinion of the champ.

"Please step away from Gigalith," she old Alder. "Look at the property damage it has created. I have no choice but to take it into custody."

"That is not necessary," protested Alder. "Gigalith's done with being upset!"

Officer Jenny refused to bend the rules. Before she could take hold of the Pokémon, a damaged statue started to topple towards her.

"Help!" she screamed, as Gigalith leap up and knocked her to the ground.

When the dust clouds cleared, the courageous Pokémon stood above the officer, shielding her from falling rubble. It was a brave, selfless act that revealed the true beauty of Gigalith's nature.

"Gigalith wants to know if you're OK?" winked Alder.

Officer Jenny was shaken, but unhurt — Gigalith had saved her life!

"I'm fine," she replied. "Thank you!"

"Why not head home Gigalith?" suggested Alder. "Jenny, are you good with that?"

Jenny saluted gratefully.

"Yes, sir!"

As Gigalith disappeared into the distance, Ash asked Alder to finish what he had been telling him at the Pokémon Center.

"You were asking us if strength was all we needed," the Trainer prompted, noticing the champ's blank face.

"Oh yes!" said Alder. "Of course I want to become strong, but I also want people who see me battle to grow closer to Pokémon, just as I want Pokémon to grow closer to people! That's the kind of battling that I live for."
Ash's face lit up.

"People liking Pokémon..." he chorused. "and Pokémon liking people!" piped up Iris.

"The one thing that matters most to me is people and Pokémon working together with mutual respect," nodded Alder. "Living in perfect harmony!"
Ash, Iris and Cilan were very impressed – they liked the idea of Pokémon and people working things out together.

"Remember that there are many different types of Trainer however," added Alder. "There's no one right answer."

Ash decided that it was time to cross the Driftveil Drawbridge. He hoped with all his heart that as his travels continued, he would find more answers, too!

"Make your journey a safe one," said Alder, walking to the edge of Nimbasa City to wave the youngsters off.

"Not being reckless is best," Cilan nodded seriously, "safety first you know!"
Alder threw back his head and roared with laughter.

"I guess you got me there!" he guffawed. "Live life to the fullest anyway! See you again! Please give Tristan my best when you meet him next!"

"Right!" replied Ash, waving.
He thought of Trip and smiled. Alder had taught him a valuable lesson that he would never forget. Ash didn't know where his journey would take him, but he was determined to have fun along the way! The Trainer took a deep breath, then placed his first step on the Driftveil Drawbridge.

Once again, our heroes have experienced the all-important bond between people and Pokémon. This time they owe a debt of thanks to their new friend, Unova League Champion Alder!

POKÉMON™

Colour in this awesome poster using all of your favourite shades. Which Pokémon would you most like to have battling on your side? The choice is yours!

ANSWERS

Page 14 - Watch Your Back!
1.

TIMBURR

2.

MIENFOO

3.

SAWK

Page 15 - Titans Of Unova

Page 16 - Evolution Revolutions
1. PETILIL – LILLIGANT
2. ROGGENROLA – BOLDORE – GIGALITH
3. AXEW – FRAXURE – HAXORUS
4. MUNNA – MUSHARNA

5. KLINK – KLANG – KLINKLANG
6. EMOLGA
7. DEINO – ZWEILOUS – HYDREIGON
8. TYMPOLE – PALPITOAD – SEISMITOAD

Pages 18-19 - Cilan's Connoisseur Quiz
1. c
2. a
3. a
4. c
5. b
6. a
7. c
8. b
9. a
10. b

Pages 30-31 - Pokémon Picture Wordsearch

K	R	O	O	K	O	D	I	L	E	G	G
D	L	K	T	E	L	F	F	U	R	A	S
E	F	P	J	G	F	J	B	X	Z	L	X
L	X	D	V	N	S	A	Y	P	N	V	C
D	V	C	G	I	W	O	A	S	I	A	B
D	W	L	O	L	H	R	W	J	G	N	K
A	B	Q	I	R	A	O	Q	T	J	T	N
W	N	B	G	E	S	R	R	C	M	U	E
E	M	Z	S	E	C	D	X	H	Z	L	H
S	N	N	T	D	N	M	C	P	T	A	C
D	A	R	M	A	N	I	T	A	N	F	R
P	U	R	R	L	O	I	N	S	S	Q	A

1. PURRLOIN
2. KROOKODILE
3. ARCHEN
4. THROH
5. DARMANITAN
6. SEWADDLE
7. GALVANTULA
8. RUFFLET
9. DEERLING
10. PANSEAR

76

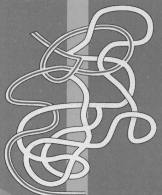

ANSWERS